"The Fire Between Us Is Still There.

"Nothing has changed, Liza."

"You're wrong, Jacques. Everything has changed."

"I don't think so. Let me prove it to you."

"No!"

Jacques looked at Liza. She still wanted him, he told himself as he fought the dark storm of emotion her denial had set whirling inside him. Regardless of her protests, the fire between them burned just as hot, just as fiercely, as it had three years ago. And he intended it to burn again.

It had to. He wanted to be free of hoping, of wanting more. And he wanted to be free of her. Liza could give him that freedom and he would give her hers by sating their physical need for one another until the white-hot flame burned itself out.

And when it was over, this time he would be the one to walk away without looking back.

Dear Reader,

Happy Valentine's Day! This season of love is so exciting for us here at Silhouette Desire that we decided to create a special cover treatment for each of this month's love stories—just to show how much this very romantic holiday means to us.

And what a fabulous group of books we have for you! Let's start with Joan Elliott Pickart's MAN OF THE MONTH, *Texas Moon*. It's romantic and wonderful—and has a terrific hero!

The romance continues with Cindy Gerard's sensuous *A Bride for Abel Greene*, the next in her NORTHERN LIGHTS BRIDES series, and also with Elizabeth Bevarly's *Roxy and the Rich Man*, which launches her new miniseries about siblings who were separated at birth, THE FAMILY McCORMICK.

Christine Pacheco is up next with *Lovers Only*, an emotional and compelling reunion story. And Metsy Hingle's dramatic writing style shines through in her latest, *Lovechild*.

It's always a special moment when a writer reaches her 25the book milestone—and that's just what Rita Rainville has done in the humorous and delightful Western, *City Girls Need Not Apply*.

Silhouette Desire—where you will always find the very best love stories! Enjoy them all....

Lucia Macro

Senior Editor

Please address questions and book requests to:
Silhouette Reader Service
U.S.: 3010 Walden Ave., P.O. Box 1325, Buffalo, NY 14269
Canadian: P.O. Box 609, Fort Erie, Ont. L2A 5X3

METSY HINGLE

LOVECHILD

SILHOUETTE *Desire*

Published by Silhouette Books

America's Publisher of Contemporary Romance

SILHOUETTE BOOKS

ISBN 0-373-76055-8

LOVECHILD

Books by Metsy Hingle

Silhouette Desire

Seduced #900
Surrender #978
Backfire #1026
Lovechild #1055

METSY HINGLE

is a native of New Orleans who loves the city in which she grew up. She credits the charm of her birthplace, and her own French heritage, with instilling in her the desire to write. Married and the mother of four children, she believes in romance and happy endings. Becoming a Silhouette author is a long-cherished dream come true for Metsy and one happy ending that she continues to celebrate with each new story she writes. She loves hearing from readers. Write to Metsy at P.O. Box 3224, Covington, LA 70433.

For my husband, Jim,
and my sons, Jimmy and Stephen—
the three special heroes in my own life
who dispel the darkness with their love.

One

He had been set up!

The realization held the sobering sting of an open-palmed slap and none of the satisfaction of having earned it. Jacques Gaston rubbed his jaw, feeling the force of the blow just as effectively as if he had been smacked across the face.

Only this time the crack to his cheek hadn't been delivered by his drunken father or by an angry female who had refused to believe he'd meant it when he had told her he would share his bed but never his heart. No, this time the head-ringing clip had been delivered by Aimee and Peter Gallagher—the two people he had considered his best friends.

And they had delivered the sucker punch in the form of Liza O'Malley.

Liza.

Jacques gave himself a mental kick for his gullibility. He had no doubts whatsoever that his so-called friends had known she would be here. They had played him like a finely tuned Stradivarius, knowing he would agree to serve in their steads on the Art For Kids' Sake Committee the moment Aimee had told him her pregnancy precluded them traveling to Chicago. As Aimee had pointed out, his guest-artist lecture series would coincide conveniently with the final stages of the fund-raising campaign. Serving on the committee would require only a few hours of his time at meetings and a handful of fund-raising events, Aimee had told him. And just as conveniently it would throw him and Liza together again.

Ah, Aimee, mon amie, *despite my silence, you knew, didn't you? That the fires had burned between me and Liza. And now you think to rekindle them? To save me from what you see as my life of loneliness? But it is too late. It was always too late.*

Even with Liza.

Especially with Liza.

Ignoring the sudden tightness in his chest, Jacques continued to stare at the woman he had tried so hard to forget. He noted the long swath of golden hair swishing like silk at her shoulders as she moved, the lush green eyes the color of new leaves on a vine in his family's vineyard. She was even more beautiful now than he remembered.

And he had had three long years to remember her, to think of her exquisite face, to recall the softness of her lithe body. The three years slipped away in the space of a heart-beat, sending him back to that last night of passion when she had professed her love for him. Back to that night when he had found himself teetering on the brink between heaven and hell as he allowed himself to contemplate the danger, to even dare and hope that he might be able to share his life with someone. To share his life with *her.*

Mon Dieu! Jacques clamped down on the surge of emotions that seeing her had unearthed inside him. Ignoring the hum of voices and the people who meandered about the room, he moved toward the window and concentrated on steadying his breathing. Snow fluttered outside, dancing before the high-rise's expanse of windows. But the memories clutched at his throat, choking him, sending him back to the oppressive heat of that autumn in New Orleans three years ago. Back to that night when she had quietly slipped from his bed and his life—like a thief in the night—without explanation, without even a goodbye and taken with her a chunk of his heart.

I'm over her, he told himself, turning away from the window. He watched her move about the room with the same inherent grace and sensuality that had captivated him so completely three years ago. Seduction in a copper suede suit, he thought wryly, as desire stirred inside him.

Un fou, Jacques swore silently. He *was* a fool. Worse, he had lied to himself. Even after all this time he hadn't forgotten her, nor had his body.

As though sensing his gaze, Liza turned. The smile on her lips wavered. Her fair skin lost even more color. Judging by the stunned look on her face, Liza O'Malley had not forgotten him, either.

Play it smart, Gaston. Do yourself a favor and get the hell out of here now, the voice inside him whispered.

But he knew he wasn't going to play it smart. Because playing it smart would mean walking away from those captivating green eyes and that soft, pouty mouth. Desire flickered inside him once more, heating his blood. But this time he didn't fight it as he recalled how those eyes had darkened when he'd kissed the sensitive spot inside her thigh, how those lips felt on his skin.

When she had first met him, Liza had called him a rogue, a gigolo. He saw no reason now not to live up to her opinion. Smiling to himself, he closed the space between them. "Hello, Liza."

"Jacques," she said his name in a breathless whisper that triggered other memories and sent him tumbling back into the past. Back to those frantic weeks after she had first disappeared and his desperation as he'd tried to find her. Anger, old yet surprisingly raw, bubbled inside him as he remembered coming to the inevitable conclusion: she didn't want to be found. She didn't want him.

Even knowing that, it had taken him months before her face, the sound of her voice, the feel of her body had stopped haunting him. Jacques curled his hands into fists as he remembered that dark period after she'd left him.

But he had gotten over her, Jacques reminded himself. He had rid himself of her betrayal just as he had rid himself of those dark, early years in France. Time had allowed him to relegate their affair to a sweet memory to be savored in his old age.

Until today.

"What a surprise," she said, her voice growing cooler as she regained her composure.

"A pleasant one I hope."

"Of course." Her tone dropped several degrees to match the snow falling outside. Her expression still wary, she extended her hand.

Her cool-as-ice manner set off other memories of how she had tried to discourage him the first time they had met by employing that "duchess to serf" technique. It was just as ineffective now as it had been then. Smiling, Jacques brushed his lips across her knuckles and enjoyed a small measure of satisfaction at the slight tremor in her fingers.

When she would have pulled her hand free, Jacques tugged her closer. Ignoring the stiffening of her spine, he leaned closer and kissed one cheek, then moved to the other. Slowly he pressed his lips against her sweet-smelling skin.

He had wanted to unnerve her, to shatter that icy calm she wore like a shield. Instead, he found himself cursing the new flickers of heat in his gut that her scent evoked.

Refusing to back off, even if it meant his getting singed

in the process, Jacques tucked a strand of hair behind Liza's ear. He drew his fingertip along her neck. Her pulse quickened at his touch and Jacques smiled, pleased by her reaction. "It has been a long time, *ma chérie.*"

"Yes, it has," she said, her voice a shade less steady as she pulled back. "What are you doing here?"

"I'm here to meet with the board members of the Art For Kids' Sake Committee."

"But you can't. I mean, this is a closed meeting for board members only."

"Then I am in the right place."

"But you're not on the board."

"Ah, but I am," Jacques insisted. "As of last night."

"That's impossible. The committee's board was formed almost a year ago, and we're already in the final stages of our fund-raising campaign," she explained. "While I appreciate your offer to serve, as will the rest of the committee, it's really too late to take on any new members, Jacques. Even you. Obviously there's been a mistake."

"It is no mistake, *ma chérie.*" Jacques grinned as her lips thinned at the familiar endearment.

"Then a misunderstanding," she countered. "There are no openings on the board. But if you're interested in serving as a volunteer for some of the fund-raising activities, I'll be happy to put you in touch with the right person. In fact, I'll introduce you to Jane Burke right now. She's the one who's in charge of—"

Jacques caught her arm as she started to turn away. "Liza, there is no mistake. I *am* on the committee's board. I am filling in for Peter."

"But—"

"He and Aimee could not be here. And you know what a stickler Peter is about fulfilling his responsibilities. He asked me to take his place. And I agreed." No point in telling her that he now suspected it had all been a con job to get Liza and him together again.

Alarm clouded her eyes. "Is something wrong with Aimee? Is there a problem with the baby?"

"Aimee is fine. And so is the baby," he assured her, giving her arm a light squeeze. "But according to our friends, this pregnancy has been more difficult than the last one, and Aimee's doctor thinks it is better for her not to travel right now."

"I see."

Jacques wanted to laugh as he watched her school her expression and don what he considered her "duchess" persona again. "Well, it was thoughtful of Peter to ask you to come," she continued, her tone becoming all business. "But it's really not necessary. Everything's under control on this end. I'll let Peter know that it's not necessary for you to take his place on the board."

Jacques tossed back his head and laughed. "I see you have not lost your touch, *ma chérie*. In fact, you have gotten even better at it."

Liza frowned. "Gotten better at what?"

"At cutting a man off at his knees, letting him know what little need you have for him."

"I do no such thing," she tossed back.

"Of course you do. You push that pretty little nose of yours up in the air and make your eyes go all frosty with that regal expression...."

"Really, Jacques, I—"

"Yes. That is it. That is the look I am talking about," he told her grinning. "It always amazed me the way you could tell a man to 'get lost' without even opening your pretty mouth."

Liza's lips thinned. The look she shot him would have melted a glacier. "Then perhaps you would be wise to heed the message."

"Ah, that too has not changed."

She arched her brow imperiously.

"When the look does not work, you use that sharp tongue of yours to finish the job."

"Honestly, Jacques. You've quite an imagination. Perhaps you should consider writing fantasies instead of sculpting."

Jacques allowed the smile to spread across his face as he moved his gaze from her mouth to her eyes. "If you will recall, sweet Liza, sometimes my sculpting *has* led to the creation of fantasies. You, yourself, helped me with one of my most memorable ones."

A rush of color raced up her cheeks at the reminder of the afternoon when he'd given Liza her first sculpting lesson and how that lesson had ended—in a maelstrom of frenzied lovemaking that had left them both exhausted and wanting more of each other.

"I see you *do* remember," he said, pleased by her reaction.

"And I see you haven't changed. A gentleman wouldn't deliberately attempt to embarrass someone this way."

"But, *ma chérie,* have you forgotten? I am no gentleman. I am a Frenchman."

The look she shot him could have turned flames to ice. Jacques chuckled, only making her expression grow even more chilly. "You would do better to save your wintry glares for someone else, Liza. They did not work on me three years ago, and they certainly will not work on me now. I have grown—how do you Americans say—? 'a thicker skin.'"

"And evidently an even bigger ego."

"I will take that as a compliment."

"It wasn't meant as one."

Jacques took her hand and raised it to his lips. He kissed her fingers and enjoyed seeing the cool facade slip a notch. Suddenly the need to bait her, to force a reaction from her, withered at the feel of her soft skin. Desire took its place. It swirled around him, covering him like mist. "Then I guess I will have to try to change your opinion of me. Perhaps by working with you on this fund-raiser, you will discover something in me that is worthy of your praise."

Something flickered in her eyes. Pain? Regret? Longing? Or was it his own feelings he saw reflected there?

"Jacques, I—"

"There you are, Liza. I wondered where you had disappeared to."

Jacques stiffened at the sound of the man's voice.

Liza pulled her hand free and turned toward the approaching man. "Oh, Robert. I'm so sorry. I'm afraid I forgot all about asking for coffee to be sent in."

"Don't worry about it. It's been taken care of. I suspected you got sidetracked when you didn't come back." He turned to Jacques and flashed him a smile of perfect white teeth. "Robert Carstairs. I'm the Art For Kids' Sake committee's co-director," he said, extending his hand.

"Jacques Gaston, your new co-director."

At Carstairs's lifted brow, Liza explained, "Jacques is filling in for Peter. The Gallaghers aren't going to be able to take part in the fund-raising activities this year, after all. Peter has asked Jacques to take his place on the committee. Jacques is an old friend of the Gallaghers'."

"And of Liza's," Jacques amended, shaking the other man's hand.

"Always happy to meet a friend of the Gallaghers' and Liza's."

Custom-made suit, soft hands, old money, Jacques sized up the other man. And given the warmth in the other man's expression when his gaze lingered on Liza, his interest in her went beyond the committee's fund-raising endeavors. For some reason the realization irritated Jacques, and he found himself biting back the urge to put a proprietary arm around Liza and draw her closer to him.

"Gaston," Carstairs repeated. He narrowed his eyes as

he continued to study Jacques. "Gaston. Gaston. Why does that name sound so familiar?"

"Perhaps Liza has mentioned our friendship," Jacques offered, earning a scowl from Liza.

"Jacques is an artist," Liza explained. "Some of his work has been on display at Gallagher's Gallery in the past. You've probably seen it there."

"Of course. Now I remember," Carstairs smiled again as recognition dawned. "You're the sculptor."

"One and the same," Jacques acknowledged with a flourish.

"Liza's right, of course. I have seen your work. Very impressive."

"I like to think so," Jacques replied, seeing no need for false modesty.

"As you can see," Liza said, her voice tinged with sarcasm, "Jacques doesn't suffer from any lack of self-confidence."

Carstairs chuckled. "Don't be too rough on him, Liza. Confidence is not such a bad thing to have. In your case, Gaston, I expect it's probably warranted. I caught your exhibit at Gallagher's Gallery last spring. As I said, it was most impressive. There was one piece in particular, a nude of a woman. It was stunning. I must admit I was quite taken with it."

"Thank you," Jacques said, inclining his head. "I know the piece you mean. *La Femme*. Woman," he said, translating. "It is one of my favorites."

A grin tugged at Carstairs's lips that said, as a man he could certainly understand why. "I guess that explains why my offer to buy it was turned down."

"Yours is not the first offer I have refused for her. The piece is part of my personal collection and not for sale. Usually I do not even allow it to be shown. But Peter caught me in a weak moment and I agreed."

"Perhaps I can catch you in another one and convince

you to sell it to me. As I said, I was truly captivated by the piece. And I'd still like to add it to my collection. I can promise you my offer would be most generous.''

Even if Jacques hadn't had an abhorrence for rich fools who thought everything and everyone had a price, he would have disliked Robert Carstairs simply for the covetous way he looked at Liza.

''Think about it.'' He pulled a business card out of an engraved gold case and offered it to Jacques. ''And let me know if you change your mind.''

''I won't.'' Ignoring the card, Jacques used the three-inch advantage his own six feet four inches gave him over Carstairs to look down at the other man. ''You see, I was quite enamored with the model who posed for it.''

''I can certainly see how you might have been,'' Carstairs told him, giving him another man-to-man look. ''By the same token, it would be a shame to let sentiment get in the way of a good business deal.''

''True. But then, the lady who posed for *La Femme* had nothing to do with business. She was very special to me.'' His gaze shifted to Liza, remembering that humid October afternoon in New Orleans when she had posed for him and he had recreated her body in clay. He allowed his gaze to slide over her, recalling how his hands, covered in damp clay, had moved over her soft curves molding the swell of her breasts, shaping the round curve of her hips, the tender apex at her thighs.

Suddenly the two of them were back in the tiny loft with the hot sun pouring through the window, bathing Liza in its glow, heating the room and their bodies while desire simmered in their blood. Liza stood naked before him, and he stripped off his own shirt in deference to the relentless heat.

''Jacques,'' his name was a soft gasp on her lips as he stroked the tip of her breast. Her body quivered beneath his touch.

"Maybe I should create my own sculpture," she whispered. Reaching down, she slid her hands into the mound of moist clay, warmed the mixture with her fingertips. Her lips parted in a slow smile of invitation and womanly seduction as she held her hands out in front of him. Passion, hot and sweet, gleamed in her eyes as she slowly smoothed her fingers down his throat, along his shoulder, his chest.

Jacques groaned. Desire shuddered through him as her nails scraped across his nipples, followed the trail of hair down his stomach to the snap of his jeans.

Jerking his thoughts from the past, Jacques tried to stem the fierce ache they triggered inside him. He met Liza's gaze. Desire, pure and hot, blazed in their depths, turning her eyes the color of priceless emeralds. She remembered, too, he thought, rocked by the pleasure of that discovery.

"Like I said, Gaston..."

Liza swallowed, feeling as though the air in her lungs had suddenly become shallow. Her skin felt hot and cool at the same time. There had been a chill in the room when she had first arrived for the meeting. Now the place felt like a furnace. Her stomach, already a mass of tangled knots at the shock of seeing Jacques again, did another somersault.

She was aware of the two men talking, but her brain seemed unable to register their words. Unable to stop herself, she took in the sight of Jacques.

It had been three years since she'd run away from him, fled to the Chicago area and carved out a new life and a home for herself. But for Jacques the clock had stood still.

His hair was still the color of sun-kissed wheat. Thick and untamed, it was combed away from his forehead. His face was the same slash of angles and high cheekbones, giving him that air of darkness and danger despite his coloring. His mouth, full and sensual, was still the lethal weapon she remembered. With a simple smile he had always charmed without trying, drew women to him like flies to honey and made her own knees go weak.

But it had always been Jacques's eyes, brown with flecks of gold, that she had found most fascinating. He had only to look at her to evoke the images of his hands and mouth touching her, making love to her.

As though sensing her scrutiny, Jacques sliced a glance at her. His eyes shimmered with heat as he moved them over her face, down her body and back to her lips. The impact was just as effective as a bold caress.

Liza caught her breath, unable to breathe, unable to think as the memories swamped her. Then his lips curved in a knowing smile.

Damn you, Jacques Gaston. Liza jerked her gaze away. From the smug look on his face, he had known just what she had been thinking, what memories his presence and comments had roused. Irritated with herself, Liza shook off the last vestiges of the memories and focused her attention on Robert.

"In any case if you should change your mind, give me a call." Robert pressed his business card into the palm of Jacques's hand. After glancing at his watch, he turned to Liza. "We probably should get this meeting underway. Don't you think?"

"Yes, of course," Liza said, dismayed at how surprisingly weak her voice sounded. She cleared her throat. "Why don't you go ahead and take your seat at the table, Robert. I'll be there in a moment. I'd like to have a word with Jacques."

"Fine," Carstairs replied. "Nice to have you aboard, Gaston."

When the other man was gone, a fresh bout of nerves attacked her system. Annoyed with herself for her response to Jacques's presence, Liza took a deep, calming breath and released it, then turned to face him again. Marshaling her most businesslike voice, she said, "I'll get right to the point, Jacques. There's really no need for you to stay for this meeting. I'm sure you would find it to be a waste of your time. So, I—''

"A waste of my time?" he repeated. "Peter and Aimee tell me the work your committee does is very important."

"It is, but—"

"Then, it would not be a waste of my time to help."

"You would find it boring," she insisted.

He smiled, the movement caused the dimple in his cheek to wink in a rakish way that had always made Liza's pulse scatter. It did so again. "I doubt that I would find anything where you are concerned boring, *ma chérie*."

"Please stop calling me that!"

"Ma chérie?"

"Yes," Liza hissed, her nerves growing more frayed by the second.

"It means my darling—"

"I know what it means. Just please stop calling me that." He had explained the endearment the first time they had made love. She squeezed her eyes shut for a moment, striving to regain her composure despite the pounding in her head. Opening her eyes, Liza stemmed the urge to massage her temples. "I'm sorry," she said more calmly. "Seeing you today has been a bit of a shock."

"For me as well," he told her, his expression growing serious for the first time. "Those first few weeks after you had left and I could not find you, I was frantic. I was afraid I would never see you again. Later, once I realized you did not wish for me to find you," he continued, his voice growing hard, void of the carefree and seductive charm, "I simply hoped I would not."

Liza fought the urge to wince. She didn't want his comment to hurt. She had prayed that if fate ever caused their paths to cross again, seeing him wouldn't hurt.

The prayers hadn't worked. She tucked the pain away, vowing to deal with it later—when she was alone. "I'll give Aimee and Peter a call this evening and explain that everything is under control where the committee is concerned and have them release you from your promise to serve on the board.'' She forced a smile that she knew was overbright and probably looked just as phony. It was the best she could manage at the moment. ''Goodbye, Jacques,'' she said. ''And good luck.''

''At least this time you have managed to say goodbye.''

Liza sucked in her breath, feeling the slash of his words like a knife. ''I guess I deserved that. Whether you believe me or not, I never meant to hurt you. In truth, I didn't think my leaving could hurt you.''

''Well, you were wrong.''

At the hardness in his voice, Liza wondered not for the first time if she had made a mistake by following her instincts to flee as she had. But what else could she have done? The truth hadn't been an option. It still wasn't. Besides, it was far too late for second-guessing herself.

''No comment, Liza? You have always been quite good with words. Surely you have something more to say. Some explanation.''

She tipped up her chin, refusing to allow him to goad her like this. ''What would be the point? I could tell you I'm sorry, but somehow I don't think that would be enough.''

''You are right. Pretty words would not be enough. Especially not now. Not when I have discovered that despite the way you used me, the way you lied to me,'' he said, his voice even more dangerous because it had dropped to a whisper. ''Despite everything you have done, I still want you. I want you every bit as much now as I did three years ago. Perhaps more. Because this time I know what it will be like between us.''

A shiver of pleasure skittered down Liza's spine, despite the fear his words evoked. It was a pleasure she couldn't risk. ''You don't want me, Jacques. You want revenge because I bruised that oversized ego of yours by being the one to end things between us before you did. Well, I'm afraid you're out of luck. I'm not going to give you a chance for revenge. What we had was over a long time ago. It's better if we forget it and just leave it in the past where it belongs.''

"But it is not in the past. We both know that." He stepped a fraction closer. "The passion is still there between us, *ma chérie,* like the embers of a fire that have been fanned back to a hot blaze.''

"You're wrong," Liza said, swallowing.

"Am I?''

Her heart thudded in her chest as he moved another step closer. Liza had to fight the urge to step back. To do so would be a sign of weakness, would give credence to what he was saying. Instead she tipped up her chin and met his gaze. "Yes. You're wrong.''

"I do not think so." He smiled, causing the dimple in his cheek to wink at her again. "And despite your generous offer to free me from my promise to Aimee and Peter, I think I will decline. I will be here in your city for the next six weeks for my lecture series anyway, so I will work with you and your committee.''

"Suit yourself," she said, grateful to hear the tap on the microphone and Robert calling the meeting to order.

"As you may remember, I generally do." Smiling, Jacques reached out and traced his finger along the lapel of her jacket. "And it suits me that you and I will be seeing a lot of each other while I am working on your committee.''

"I wouldn't count on it," she said, her voice flat as she stepped away from his touch.

"Ah, but I am counting on it, *ma chérie.* In fact, I am looking forward to it.''

TWO

"**D**on't forget, we'll be sending out the invitations for the auction and dinner dance the first week of December," Liza reminded the board members, while she carefully avoided looking at Jacques. But it didn't stop her from being aware of him. How could she not be? Even without their past history, he would have been difficult to ignore. He had asked intelligent questions, offered good suggestions and had charmed the socks off the other board members. Or perhaps stockings was more appropriate, given the flurry of feminine interest that had buzzed through the room after Jacques had introduced himself.

"That means I'll need each of you to get your lists of potential ticket buyers to me as soon as possible. Of course, no one here has to wait for an official invitation. We'll be happy to take your order for tickets and your checks to-night. Remember, the more tickets we sell, the more money we raise for the summer camp for the kids." Liza smiled despite the hammerlike pounding in her head. "Once again,

I want to personally thank each of you for coming this evening and for all of your help and support. I'm looking forward to seeing each of you at the patron party next month.''

Chairs scraped across the tiled floor as the meeting disbanded. For the next ten minutes, Liza smiled and gratefully accepted ticket orders and checks.

''Great job, Liza,'' Robert said fifteen minutes later as he handed her his own check for tickets. ''Looks like we're off to a good start. Just about everyone has committed to purchase a full table for the dinner. I've never seen this group so eager to part with their money before.''

''Let's hope the rest of Chicago responds the same way.''

''They will,'' he assured her. ''With you in charge, I have no doubt about that.''

''Thank you.''

''What about my offer to buy you dinner? We could celebrate tonight's advance sales with a good bottle of wine and a nice Chateaubriand.''

Guilt lanced through Liza as she realized she had been so distracted by Jacques's presence that she'd forgotten all about Robert and his invitation to have dinner. ''Would you mind terribly if I took a rain check? I was hoping to go over my notes for the patron party tonight. I'm meeting with the caterers tomorrow.''

''Of course not,'' he said, but Liza could see the disappointment in his eyes. ''Everything okay? You don't seem yourself tonight.''

''Everything's fine. I just have a monster headache and I'm afraid I'd be lousy company.''

''You couldn't be lousy company even if you tried,'' he said, his voice filled with affection and warmth. Lines of concern etched his handsome face. ''But I think you're pushing yourself too hard. Stop worrying about the patron party and the gala. It's going to be a great success. What you need is a good night's rest.''

"You're probably right.''

"I know I am. Would you like me to drive you home? I can have your car sent to you in the morning.''

"No. I'll be okay. But thanks anyway.''

"You're sure?''

"Yes.''

He gave her hand a light squeeze. "All right. Just let me have a quick word with Harvey Adams and then I'll walk you to your car.''

What was wrong with her? Liza demanded silently as she watched him walk away. Robert Carstairs was everything she could want in a man—kind, patient and generous to a fault. Only a week ago she had convinced herself she was ready to take their friendship to the next level. After all, it had been more than three years since her affair with Jacques had ended—more than enough time to get over him. And she had thought she was over him.

Until he had walked through the door tonight. A shiver skipped down Liza's spine as she recalled the heat in his eyes when he had told her he still wanted her. Then suddenly it was as though it was only yesterday that she'd been in his arms, wild with a hunger and need that only he seemed able to fill.

No! Liza screamed silently. Drawing a deep breath, she reached for the meeting files and began packing them away. She wouldn't allow herself to fall into Jacques's sensual trap again. She couldn't. She had too much to lose—even more than she had when she'd run away three years ago.

The hum of voices grew around her, but Liza ignored them. Ordinarily she would have joined in the after-meeting chatter. She enjoyed these people, and a number of them were potential clients. In fact, she had even planned to follow up on several inquiries about her services as a fundraiser. But not tonight, she told herself, as she retrieved another handful of folders from the table and stored them in her briefcase. Not when the shock of seeing Jacques again was still so fresh. Not when she was so keenly aware of his presence in the room. She'd have to face him again. Of that much she was sure. But not yet, not before she had figured out what to do.

"I think I'm in love."

Liza looked up from the stacks of papers to Jane Burke, her friend and co-worker on the committee. At just over five feet, with jet black hair and dark eyes, Jane was her direct opposite in appearance and philosophy. The other woman was as reckless and romantic as Liza was cautious and pragmatic. Yet the two had become fast friends. "Again?" Liza asked casually, used to her friend falling in and out of love at the drop of a hat.

"Don't be snide, Liza."

"Who is it this time?"

"The committee's new co-director, Jacques Gaston." At the arch of Liza's brow, she insisted, "This time it's the real thing."

"Need I remind you that's what you said three weeks ago when you met that Bobby What's-his-name from Texas?"

"I know."

"And let's not forget about Beauregard Jefferson Davis from Mississippi."

Jane laughed, the sound light and carefree. "What can I say? I'm a sucker for a fellow with an accent." As if on cue, the deep rumble of Jacques's voice carried across the room to them. "Who could blame me? Can you imagine what it would be like to hear *him* whisper sweet nothings in your ear."

She didn't have to imagine, Liza thought at the sound of the deep voice, heavily accented by his native French. Memories came rushing back to her of those nights she'd spent wrapped in his arms, listening to his stories about the vineyard in France where he'd lived as a boy. She had envisioned him easily, a handsome boy with a devilish twinkle in his eyes, racing through the vineyard, laughing as he swiped grapes from the vines and popped them into his mouth. For a short time during their brief affair, she had even been foolish enough to fantasize that the two of them would travel there together one day. She had so wanted to see the valleys he had described to her, the place he had painted for her so vividly with his words.

But that had been before she had realized that Jacques didn't love her. That he would never permit himself to love her or any woman. And even worse that there was no place in his life or his heart for her love.

"I wonder if it's true what they say about Frenchmen," Jane murmured. "You know, about them being better lovers."

Unbidden, Liza's gaze followed her friend's to where Jacques stood flanked by three of the female board members. One of the trio murmured something to him and Jacques tossed back his head and laughed. A swift pang shot through Liza and she jerked her gaze away. "If I were you, I wouldn't be too anxious to find out—not if you still want marriage, motherhood and that white picket fence."

"Why not?"

"Because unless he's changed a great deal, you'll never have any of those things with Jacques. He's allergic to even the thought of marriage or commitment." After all, she should know, Liza added silently.

Jane wrinkled her nose. "Don't you know that no man ever *wants* to settle down? They fight it tooth and nail until the right woman comes along and changes their mind for them."

"You make marriage sound like…like taming a pet. Trust me, Jane. Jacques Gaston is no domestic house cat. And I wouldn't count on changing his mind on the subject, either. There certainly have been enough women who've tried." Not that she had been one of them. She had only wanted to love him and be loved by him. But even that had proved too much for Jacques.

"I didn't realize you knew him so well," Jane said, a curious gleam in her dark eyes.

"I don't." Despite the fact that they had been lovers, she had never really known Jacques. She had been too caught up in their passion to discover the sad, lonely man that had lain beneath the happy-go-lucky facade he presented to the world. Until it had been too late. "We met a few years ago in New Orleans while I was working for Aimee Gallagher. Jacques was one of her tenants."

"So, then you two are old friends?"

"More like adversaries. We didn't get along very well." Except for that short time when they had been lovers. But even then, their relationship had remained volatile. And despite the fact that she had fallen in love with him, she and Jacques had never quite managed to become friends. If they had, perhaps things would not have ended as they did. "We still don't."

"Adversaries, huh? I guess that explains why he's looking at you like a hungry cat eyeing a tasty little mouse."

Liza looked up. Her eyes tangled with the tawny-colored ones staring back at her. For a moment she forgot to breathe. When Jacques winked, she jerked her gaze away. "Don't read anything into it. Jacques takes his role as a Frenchman seriously. He thinks it's his duty to flirt with any female from eight to eighty."

Her friend gave her a speculative look, then went back to sorting papers. She handed Liza a pile of the agendas that had been scattered on the table. "Still, it sure would be interesting to find out if what they say about Frenchmen is true."

"And just what is it they say about Frenchmen?" Jacques asked.

Liza whipped around. Her heart thundered in her chest.

Jane's face split into a welcoming smile. "Why that they're—"

"That they're very…French," Liza offered quickly, while struggling to keep the color from crawling up her cheeks. Noting the amused look in his eyes, Liza tipped up her chin. "Jacques, I'd like you to meet Jane Burke. Jane, Jacques Gaston."

"Mademoiselle Burke." He took her hand and brought it to his lips. The other woman practically swooned.

"Jane is the person responsible for organizing the committee's volunteers," Liza continued, unsure which irritated her more, the dazzled expression on her friend's face or Jacques's easy charm. "I was explaining to Jacques earlier that it really wasn't necessary for him to take Peter's place on the board and suggested he might want to work with your group of volunteers."

"Why, of course, we would *love* to have you work with our group, Mr. Gaston."

"Jacques," he corrected.

"Jacques," she repeated, her face beaming. "And please, you must call me Jane."

"A lovely name for a lovely lady," Jacques said smoothly. "And I am sure you will understand, Jane, that as much as I would enjoy working with you, I believe my time would be better served working with Liza to ensure the success of the fund-raiser."

"Why, of course I understand," Jane agreed, her cheeks flushed. "And you're right. Despite what Liza says, I know she can use your help—especially with Peter and Aimee both out of the picture."

"Is that right?" Jacques shifted his gaze to Liza.

"Oh, yes," Jane assured him and then launched into a list of the many details for which Liza was responsible—all of which would certainly benefit from any help that Jacques would offer.

Resisting the urge to strangle both her friend and

Jacques, Liza crammed the remaining meeting paraphernalia into her briefcase. She snapped it shut and removed it from the table. "If you'll both excuse me, I need to speak with Robert about the patron party before I leave."

Ten minutes later, after declining Robert's offer to see her to her car, Liza slipped out of the meeting room. At least she had managed to avoid another encounter with Jacques, she told herself as she walked down the hallway toward the exit. Judging by the way Ashley Hartmann had been clinging to his arm when she had seen him last, he would be fully occupied for the rest of the evening.

Not that it made any difference to her, Liza decided. After all, she and Jacques were history. What he did and who he did it with were of no concern to her.

Then why did the image of the redheaded divorcée laughing up at him and clutching at his sleeve leave such a foul taste in her mouth and an achy feeling in her chest?

Because you're an idiot, Liza O'Malley. You always were, where Jacques was concerned. Frowning, Liza turned the corner and headed toward the elevators.

"Such a long face. Problem, *ma chérie?*"

Liza stopped. Her gaze shot over to where Jacques stood lounging against the wall next to the elevators. "Not at all," she finally managed to say despite the rush of nerves that tightened like a knot in her stomach. Shifting her briefcase from one hand to the other, she continued over to the bank of elevators and pushed the button for the lobby. "I'm just surprised to see you leaving so early." Or alone, she added silently.

"Why is that?"

"Well, since you're so eager to serve on the committee's board, I thought you would take advantage of this opportunity to become better acquainted with the other board members." And Ashley Hartmann in particular.

"I would much prefer reacquainting myself with the committee's fund-raising coordinator."

The elevator arrived, saving her from the need to respond. Liza stepped inside the half-filled car, and Jacques followed. The doors slid shut, enclosing them in the small space. The short ride to the lobby suddenly seemed to stretch endlessly. Even with a half dozen other people inside the car, Liza couldn't help being keenly aware of Jacques standing beside her. She could smell the scents of summer sunshine and damp clay, of pine woods and man— a unique mingling of scents that she had always associated with Jacques. And with the scents came back the memories—the feel of his hands shaping her, his mouth tasting and teasing.

Liza's breath snagged in her chest. She squeezed her eyes shut against the memory.

"Liza?"

At the sound of his voice, Liza opened her eyes immediately. Her body tense, she tightened her fingers around the handle of her briefcase.

"Is something wrong?"

"No," she said quickly.

Moments later when the elevator doors opened, she raced through them and out into the lobby.

"Liza, wait."

She kept moving down the polished corridor, eager to reach the parking garage elevator and escape Jacques and the rush of memories plaguing her.

He gripped her arm, bringing her to a halt. Gently, too gently, he caught her chin and forced her to look at him. "What is wrong? Why do you run from me?"

"I'm not running from you," she lied. "I have a headache, and I'm just anxious to get home."

He hesitated, and Liza grew uncomfortable under his probing gaze. "Then I will take you home." Still holding on to her arm, he took her briefcase from her and continued toward the parking garage elevators.

"I appreciate the offer, but it's not necessary."

"You are ill."

"I have a headache," she said, and tugged her arm free. "I promise you I can manage. Besides, I don't live in the city. 'Home' is more than an hour's drive outside of Chicago."

"I do not mind the drive."

"But I do."

"I will see you to your car," he insisted, following her into the garage elevator despite her protests.

"That really isn't necessary."

"I *said* I will see you to your car. Which floor?"

Under the harsh lighting of the elevator, his roughly hewed features and dark gold hair reminded her of a Viking warrior. The fact that he towered over her own considerable height only added to the image. But it was the determination in his leonine gaze that made her decide it was pointless to argue further. She punched the number three for her parking level.

Moments later when the doors opened, Liza stepped out into the cold, shadowed garage. Jacques walked beside her, his silence making her even more anxious. Finally she reached the dark blue sedan. "Well, this is it," she said with more cheerfulness than she was feeling. After unlocking her car and allowing him to store her briefcase on the back seat, she turned to him. "Well, thanks again."

"Aren't you at least going to offer me a ride?"

"But I thought... What about *your* car?"

His mouth kicked up at the corners in what she had always considered his lady-killer grin. "I do not have one. Peter had someone meet me at the airport when I arrived this morning, and I took a taxi to the meeting. I have not yet called the rental agency."

Liza narrowed her eyes. "And I suppose there's a reason you can't take another taxi now?"

"Perhaps I am still the struggling artist with big dreams and little money."

"We both know that's not true."

The smile in his eyes died. So did the one on his lips. "No. It is not. I have done well since our time together in New Orleans. Perhaps if my fortunes had come sooner, you would not have chosen to leave me as you did."

The words hurt, as did the bitterness she detected behind them, but Liza didn't bother to deny his accusations. It was better he thought she had deserted him because of his lack of money than for him to know the truth.

"Now it seems fate has brought us together again. I am looking forward to working with you on this fund-raiser."

Panic shot through her at his words. Liza's gaze shot up to meet his. "Why are you doing this, Jacques? What are you up to?"

"Ah. I see you are still a suspicious soul." Instead of the underlying bitterness she had detected moments earlier, she glimpsed an intensity in him that she found far more disturbing. "Surely two old friends such as you and I can work together."

"We were lovers, Jacques. Not friends."

"Yes. And you were a spectacular lover, *ma chérie*." He moved a step closer, caging her between the car door and his body. He skimmed his thumb along the line of her cheek, across her bottom lip. "So responsive."

Liza shivered, unable to quell her reaction to his touch, unable to look away.

"Did you think I had forgotten?" he asked, his voice rough with some emotion she couldn't decipher. "I wanted to. God knows I tried to forget you. But I could not. Just as I cannot stop myself from wanting you now." Heat flared in his eyes, turning them to molten gold.

And then he was lowering his head, his mouth was brushing hers, testing, tasting, tempting. His tongue traced the lines of her lips. "Open for me, Liza."

She obeyed his command, parting her lips.

Jacques groaned. The deep husky sound sent a shudder

through her. When his tongue slid inside her mouth and began an erotic mating ritual with her own, Liza heard the moan of pleasure escape from her own lips.

And then she was beyond hearing, beyond thinking. All she could do was feel. She clung to his shoulders, her head spinning as wave after wave of need lapped at her greedily, demanding more.

"Ah, Liza," he murmured as his mouth forged its way to her ear and then retraced the path back to reclaim her lips. Despite the cold temperature and threat of new snow, she was burning up inside, her body suffused with heat.

Jacques captured her face between his hands, forcing her to look at him. She could see the desire burning in his eyes and feared he would see it in hers as well.

"It is still there. The fire between us. Nothing has changed, Liza. Nothing."

Reality came back to her in a rush as the impact of his words registered. When he started to kiss her again, Liza turned her head away. "You're wrong, Jacques. Everything has changed."

"Has it?"

"Yes."

"I do not think so, *ma chérie*. Let me prove it to you."

"No!"

Something dark and dangerous flashed in his eyes. For a moment she thought he would ignore her. Then he dropped his arms and stepped back.

Still shaky, Liza turned her back to him and opened the car door. "If you still want a ride to your hotel, get in." She didn't look at him. She couldn't. Once he was strapped in the seat beside her, she asked, "Where are you staying?"

"At Peter and Aimee's apartment. It is on—"

"I know where it is," Liza told him. After all, she had often used the place herself during the past three years. In fact, she had already accepted Aimee's offer to use the guest room on the evening of the patron party and the black-tie gala next month. Of course that would no longer be an option, Liza realized as she maneuvered her car along the snow-lined streets. She would just have to make other arrangements. But having a convenient place to stay while she was in Chicago was the least of her worries now.

Jacques glanced over at Liza, noting how tightly her gloved fingers gripped the steering wheel. She still wanted him, he told himself as he fought the dark storm of emotion her denial had set whirling inside him. Regardless of her protests, the fire between them burned just as hot, just as fiercely as it had three years ago.

He intended for it to burn again.

It had to. Otherwise he would spend the rest of his life haunted by her and the foolish notion that they could have had a future together. They couldn't. It was impossible. He had to prove it to himself or he would never know peace again.

She had been right when she had accused him of wanting revenge. He did. But more than revenge he wanted to be free of hoping, of wanting more. And he wanted to be free of her. Liza could give him that freedom, and he would give her hers by sating their need for each other until the white-hot flame burned itself out.

Then there would be no more sleepless nights spent yearning for her. No more foolishly wanting to hear her words of love. No more cursing the darkness in his soul that prevented him from ever saying those same words to her or to any woman. And when it was over, he would be the one to walk away without looking back.

"This is it," Liza said, pulling up in front of the apartment building that housed the elegant penthouse suite the Gallaghers had insisted he use.

"Would you like to come upstairs for a drink?"

"No, thanks. I need to get home."

"Perhaps dinner tomorrow night, then? We can discuss the fund-raiser and old times."

She looked away from him and stared out of the window. "I'm busy."

"What about the day after tomorrow?"

"I already have plans."

Jealousy reached out, gripped him by the throat and refused to let go as he considered the possibility of those plans including Robert Carstairs. No, he told himself. She couldn't be involved with Carstairs or anyone else—not if she responded to his kiss as she did. "Then I guess I will just have to be satisfied with seeing you again on Tuesday."

Her head whipped around at his remark. Her green eyes stared at him warily. "What do you mean?"

"According to the schedule you passed out at the meeting, Tuesday is when you will be doing a tasting at the restaurant where the gala is being held and selecting items for the dinner menu." He pulled the sheet from his coat pocket on which he had circled each item on her checklist from the food tasting down to the balloon delivery the night of the big event. He handed it to Liza to inspect.

"You can't possibly plan to go to all of these meetings."

"Why not? You said anyone on the board was welcome to participate."

"I was being polite. You're not expected to attend detail meetings like these. No one on the board ever goes to those things. Only me."

"And now me," he said, smiling. Leaning across the seat, he kissed her protesting lips. "I will see you on Tuesday."

Three

Jacques looked up from the glass of Bordeaux he had ordered, sensing Liza's arrival even before she entered the room. *Mon Dieu*, but she was beautiful, he thought as she came into sight. Her pale hair gleamed like spun gold, swinging loosely about her shoulders. Dressed in a red sweater dress and matching high heels, she made him think of sweetness and sin. As the hostess directed her to the table, Jacques watched her start toward him on those long slender legs. Suddenly images flashed before him—of those legs wrapped around him, of her silken hair brushing against his bare skin.

Desire, hot and swift, shot through him. Jacques tightened his fingers around the stem of the wineglass, feeling the all-too-familiar ache in his groin. It had always been like this with Liza. From the first moment he had seen her three years before, he had been like a raw schoolboy who had just discovered the mystery of sex and the beauty of a woman's body. Their affair, her desertion and even the years without her had done nothing to diminish his response to her.

When she reached the table, Jacques stood and prayed no one noticed his obvious condition.

"Thank you," Liza told the hostess.

Nodding, the hostess said, "Mr. Newberry will be with you in a moment, Ms. O'Malley. Can I offer you something to drink while you wait?"

"I can recommend the Bordeaux," Jacques offered. "It is almost as good as the wine from my family's vineyard."

"Iced tea will be fine," Liza said, giving the other woman a smile.

"You Americans, you have no appreciation for the art of fine dining." Jacques pulled out her chair. "Hello, *ma chérie*," he said, noting the way her eyes narrowed at the endearment. Leaning over, he brushed his mouth against her cheek before he resumed his seat.

"I'm not here for a dining experience, Jacques. I'm here for a food tasting so that a decision can be made on the menu for next month's gala. It really wasn't necessary for you to be here for this."

"Ah, but it was," he told her. He took a sip of his wine and allowed himself the pleasure of simply looking at her. She looked so damn cool and neat, he had an urge to grab her and kiss her just to muss up that perfection. "Since you have refused my invitations, I am forced to use whatever opportunities are available so that the two of us can be together."

"There's no reason for us to be together." She reached for her napkin and smoothed it across her lap as the waitress served her iced tea.

"Of course, there is," he insisted. When she refused his offer of bread, he broke off a piece and began to butter it. "Otherwise, how will I be able to change your mind?"

"And exactly what is it you're trying to change my mind about?"

"Why, about resuming our affair, of course."

Liza dropped the spoon she'd picked up to stir her iced tea. She leaned forward, her gem-colored eyes stormy. "I promise you, Jacques, you and I are *not* going to resume our affair."

"As I said, I intend to change your mind."

"You're wasting your time. I am not going to change my mind. I'm not interested."

"That is what you said three years ago, too," he reminded her, looking up from the piece of buttered bread. "But this time you do not have to worry about being the one to seduce me."

Tracks of color climbed her cheeks and Jacques smiled, sure she remembered as he did that first time when she had asked him to make love to her.

"I assure you, I have no intention of worrying about something that isn't going to happen."

"Ah, but it will, my sweet Liza. Because I have every intention of seducing you."

Fire flickered in her eyes, but before she could respond, the catering manager arrived with a waiter in tow carrying a tray with salads.

Thirty minutes later as they made their way through the main course, Jacques listened to the catering director extoll the virtues of presentation and preparation of each dish, but his thoughts kept drifting back to the past. Back to a sultry, wet October night in New Orleans, racing through the dark French Quarter streets with Liza beside him....

"Come, *ma chérie*," he had said, pulling Liza out of the rain and into the stairwell of the old building that had led to their apartments. "You need to get out of those wet things before you catch a cold."

Her laughter teased and tempted him as they hurried up the stairs to her apartment. What a fool you are, Gaston, he thought, realizing how just the simple sound of her laughter could make him break out in a sweat of need and want. For a man who liked women and had enjoyed more than a casual friendship with many, never had he found himself so completely captivated by any one woman.

Until Liza.

With Liza everything was new, different. She made him feel alive, made him forget about the darkness.

She unlocked the door, then turned to face him. The smile that curved her mouth and had tempted him all through dinner faded. So did the laughter in her eyes.

"What is it, *chérie?*"

"I don't want to be alone tonight," she whispered.

His gut tightened at the unmistakable invitation in her voice, the sound having the same effect as a woman's nails gently scoring his naked flesh. Fighting the urge to act on her invitation, Jacques eyed her curiously and wondered not for the first time what had gotten into Liza tonight. Despite the chemistry between them, she had turned him down repeatedly. Then tonight, after months of verbal sparring and dismissing his advances, she had agreed to have dinner with him. And now, judging from the look in her eyes, she was offering him even more.

"You've changed your mind, haven't you?" she asked, cutting into his thoughts.

"About what?"

"About wanting me."

She started to turn away, but he caught her by the shoulders and turned her to face him. "You are wrong, Liza. I want you." Unable to resist, he traced his fingers along one incredibly soft cheek. The artist in him couldn't help but note the play of light and shadow that made her wet skin look translucent, her green eyes shine like emeralds. But the man in him saw the too-pale tone of her fair skin, the doubts and vulnerability in her eyes. "Wanting you is like breathing for me. It is something I do without thought or reason."

"Then come inside. Stay with me. Make me feel like a woman tonight."

The blood rushed to his head and then to his loins, but still he hesitated. Despite the number of women who had passed through his life and his bed, none of them had been casual. Each had been special to him, but none had asked for more than he could give. Friendship and good sex had been enough for both parties. Something inside told him that with Liza it would not be so simple for either of them.

She moved a step closer, bringing her body next to his. She touched him. He could feel the warmth of her fingers through his damp shirt as they inched their way up his chest, over his shoulders, to slip around his neck. "Please, Jacques," she murmured before pressing her mouth to his.

Jacques groaned. Wrapping his arms around her, he gave in to the sweet temptation of Liza's kiss. He had envisioned this moment for months, lusted for it, dreamed of it.

Reality was a thousand times better than the dream.

She moved her hips against him, cradling the ache in his lower body with her womanly softness. For a moment Jacques thought he would go mad. He wanted to strip her bare and bury himself in her sweet warmth. When she repeated the motion, Jacques pulled his mouth free. "Sacre bleu!" Curling his fists in her hair, he squeezed his eyes shut and struggled to breathe.

"Come inside," she whispered.

He didn't resist. He couldn't resist even if he had wanted to. He didn't want to.

The moment the door closed she was back in his arms. She pulled off his tie and unbuttoned his shirt, sending him into another tailspin of want and need. When she reached for his belt, he battled with the desire clawing at him and captured her hand. "Liza, do you know what you are doing?" he managed, his voice gruff, shaky even to his own ears.

"Yes."

Jacques looked into her passion-filled eyes, and his body trembled with a new wave of desire. Struggling to hold on to his last ounce of control, he asked, "You are sure?"

"I'm sure," she told him. "I know all about your rules, Jacques. No promises, no commitments. Passion and friendship only."

The words had been a creed he'd felt he had to live by. They'd been his only weapon to protect himself and others from the darkness inside him. But hearing those words come from Liza's lips, he suddenly became aware of the coldness of them...and even more he became aware of his own emptiness. "Yes, but—"

She placed a finger over his lips, silencing him. "I'm not asking for anything more, Jacques. I just want you to make love to me."

She released the button on his slacks and eased down the zipper. Her fingers brushed his hardened length and for a moment Jacques feared he would lose control.

She lifted her gaze to his once more. "Make me believe I'm a real woman tonight."

There was passion in her eyes. And doubt. For a fraction of a second he wondered why. Then her fingertips were touching him again, stroking him, driving all thoughts but making love to her from his mind. "Take my word for it, *chérie*. You are a real woman. And never in my life have I ever wanted any woman more than I want you right now."

"Then, show me."

The heat in her eyes, the plea in her voice, nearly pushed him over the edge. He tangled both fists in her hair and backed her against the door. He took possession of her mouth, covering her soft lips with his own. He wanted to savage her mouth, plunder it and claim her as his. Instead, he kissed her slowly, gliding his tongue along the edges of her mouth as he sought entry. When she opened to him, his tongue invaded, tangled with hers. He kissed her over and over, concentrating solely on her mouth and reveling in her sounds of pleasure. When she nipped his bottom lip, then pulled his mouth back to hers, Jacques crushed her body to him and deepened the kiss.

Moments later Liza jerked her mouth free to look into his eyes. "Show me, Jacques. Please."

Jacques shuddered at the husky note desire had given her voice. Slipping his arm beneath her knees, he lifted her into his arms and carried her into the bedroom. A small lamp at the bedside table bathed the room in a soft glow, illuminating the raindrops sliding silently down the windowpanes. A thick rose-and-green comforter stretched across the bed. Gardenia blossoms floated in a crystal dish scenting the air with its sweet fragrance. His artist's eye took in the details and dismissed them all, his every thought, his every breath filled with only Liza.

He stopped at the edge of the bed and tortured himself by releasing her and having her body slide slowly down the length of his as her feet touched the floor. Leaning her against the bed, he kissed her eyes, her cheeks, her mouth. He opened the first button on the excuse for a dress she'd been wearing and kissed the base of her throat. With a patience he hadn't known he possessed, Jacques forced himself to move slowly. Opening the buttons one by one, he took his time, kissing the skin he had bared. When the last button was free, he eased the dress from her shoulders. It fell in a puddle of shimmering green silk to the floor.

His blood pulsed with desire as he took in the sight of her womanly curves covered only by scraps of black lace. "God, but you are beautiful," he whispered and proceeded to worship her with his mouth and hands. He unhooked her bra and feasted on the fullness of her breasts—first with his eyes, then with his fingers as he cupped and shaped her. He caught one dark rosy nipple between his thumb and forefinger, while he lowered his head to her other breast.

Liza moaned. She clutched at his shoulders when his

mouth closed over the other crest, tugging at the tip with his teeth, then laving it with his tongue.

"Jacques!" Her fingernails bit into his skin as he moved his mouth to pay homage to her other breast, her whimpers of pleasure fueling his own desire.

He lifted her, placed her on the bed and then joined her. He slipped his hand beneath the black lace to thread his fingers through the pale triangle of curls between her legs. Easing first one finger inside her tight channel and then another, he gently stroked her.

Liza gasped. Her body shuddered and she lifted herself against his hand as he increased the rhythm and pressure.

"That is it, *chérie*," he encouraged, his own voice ragged with need as he felt the first spasms hit her, sending her honeyed warmth to flow onto his fingers. When her body went limp, he began the slow stroking again.

"Jacques, no. I can't...I...not without you."

"For me, Liza. Let go for me." Ignoring her cries, he brought her to the peak, again and again, extending his own pleasure and pain as he watched her come apart for him. When he could wait no longer, he stripped off his clothes and moved between her thighs.

The rain beat fiercely against the window, matching the frantic pace of his pulse. He ripped open the foil packet with his teeth.

"You don't need that," Liza told him. She took the packet from his fingers and tossed it to the floor.

"What about protection?" he managed to say, as she closed her fist around him.

"I can't..." Her voice broke and her eyes shimmered a moment, before she continued. "It's a safe time for me. I can't...I won't get pregnant."

He started to argue. To tell her he didn't want to take any chances. But then she was opening herself, guiding him into her heat.

"Just to be safe—"

But then she was drawing him deeper inside her, arching her body, lifting her hips. And he forgot about arguing. He forgot about thinking. All he could do was feel.

He drove himself into her, unable to wait any longer.

"Jacques."

He slid his tongue into her mouth, mimicking the movements of their bodies with the length and speed of each stroke. Then she was tearing her mouth free, wrapping her legs around him. Lightning flashed outside the window, thunder exploded in the distance, rocking the building.

Jacques watched in wonder as the first storm of pleasure hit Liza. Then she was crying out, convulsing around him and he was racing to join her in the storm—

"What about the chocolate mousse?" Liza was saying. "Do you think it's a safe choice or should we stick with the fruit compote?"

Jacques jerked his attention back to the present. He gave himself a mental shake to clear his head of the seductive memory, realizing he didn't have a clue as to what they were discussing.

"If neither of those appeal to you, the chef also does a wonderful strawberry cheesecake," Mr. Newberry offered.

Jacques looked down at the chocolate mousse and fruit compote before him. Dessert. They had been talking about dessert, Jacques concluded. "Both of these look excellent, but why don't we try a slice of that cheesecake before we decide," he said in an effort to buy time.

"Really, Jacques. Do you think that's necessary?" Liza asked, anxious to end the meal and this meeting with Jacques. She offered the catering manager a smile. "Either one of these would make a wonderful choice. Besides, I don't think I can eat another bite."

"Then just make it one slice, Mr. Newberry. Ms. O'Malley and I can share."

"Of course," the catering manager replied, and was off to do Jacques's bidding before Liza could object further.

Liza wasn't sure which disturbed her more—the intimacy implied by Jacques's insistence that they share the same dessert or by his unusually quiet mood throughout the meal. After his earlier declaration to seduce her, she had felt like a mouse waiting for the cat to pounce. While she had been glad that he hadn't pursued the subject, for some reason his reflective silence made her even more edgy.

Irritated with herself for her reaction to him, Liza focused on her purpose for being with Jacques in the first place—the gala dinner. "For starters, I think the Caesar salad would be the best choice. Don't you?"

"Yes. The Caesar salad," Jacques said without any enthusiasm whatsoever.

Liza hesitated a moment and then continued. "And for the entrée, I thought we could offer a choice of fish or the filet mignon. That way anyone who didn't want meat would have an alternative. What do you think?"

"It sounds fine to me," Jacques said, his attention still focused on his half-filled wineglass.

Liza frowned, not sure what to make of his distracted manner. Jacques had always been a connoisseur of life in general, enjoying everything he ate, drank or did with a lust that she had envied. How many times had she marveled at his ability to turn the simplest of meals into a sensuous feast? Suddenly she wondered if his lack of interest meant he disagreed with her choices and simply hadn't bothered to tell her so. "If you think I'm making a mistake, Jacques, now's the time to tell me," she said with more heat in her voice than she had intended. "I'd rather know now while I can still fix it than make a mess of things next month."

Jacques shifted his gaze to her, his expression puzzled. "There is nothing wrong with your choices, Liza. You have always had impeccable taste. Why would you think otherwise?"

"Maybe because the Jacques Gaston I used to know had a very healthy appetite. Yet you barely touched your meal and you never even tasted the desserts."

He paused for long moments, only adding to Liza's sense of uneasiness. "Perhaps, I am not the same Jacques Gaston you once knew," he said, his voice taking on a deeper, more intimate tone that raced along her nerve endings like a caress. "Or perhaps it is not food that I hunger for."

Liza's pulse stuttered, then began to race at a frenzied pace at the sensual hunger in his eyes. She curled her fingers into the napkin on her lap, feeling the traitorous heat pool between her thighs as she responded to him. She took a sip of water to clear her too-dry throat. "Food is the only thing on the menu," she quipped, feigning a calm she was far from feeling. "As soon as we make a decision on the dessert and wines, we can leave."

The waiter placed the slice of strawberry-glazed cheesecake between them and positioned forks on either side. "That is another of the foibles of you Americans. You are always in such a hurry. Never taking the time to enjoy life and its pleasures. For instance, there is no reason for us to hurry through our meal. When I spoke with Aimee and Peter, they said—"

Liza blinked. "You spoke to Aimee and Peter?"

"Yes."

"When?" She had been trying to reach the couple all weekend—without success.

"Last night. They send their love by the way," he added, smiling. "As I was saying, I understand from Aimee that when you take on a fund-raising project such as this one, it becomes your job until the project is completed. So there is no reason you must hurry back to your office. You are, in essence, working right now."

"There is every reason for me to get back to the office. There are dozens of things that still need to be taken care of, including the patron party in a few weeks."

"And I am sure you will handle them all without any trouble." Jacques sank his fork into the creamy calorie-laden confection and offered it to her.

Ignoring his offering, Liza picked up the other fork and took a bite. She couldn't taste a thing. It was a sin, she decided as she took a second bite, to ingest all these calories and not even enjoy them. And it was all Jacques's fault—for making her question her decisions, for coming back into her life and stirring up old feelings, for making her want him again when she knew any relationship between them was impossible.

"Peter tells me you are quite good at this raising of funds."

She pulled her gaze away from the sight of Jacques's mouth as he savored the cheesecake. "I hope he's right. The Art For Kids' Sake is my biggest project so far."

"Peter is a good businessman. I am sure he would not have hired you if he did not think you could do the job."

Liza had to grin at that. "Oh, I think it's safe to say Aimee may have twisted his arm a bit."

Jacques shook his head. "No. Not if Peter did not agree with her. Peter can be quite stubborn when it comes to business."

"Yes," Liza agreed, remembering the rough time her friend had gone through before Peter had been able to accept the fact that Aimee truly loved Peter for himself. It had been during that bumpy period, when Jacques had proven himself to be a true friend to Aimee, that Liza had found herself falling in love with Jacques. "Peter's the one who suggested I go out on my own and sell my skills as a professional fund-raiser."

"When was that?"

"Almost three years ago."

"So this is where you came when you left New Orleans?"

"Yes." Liza broke off another bite of cheesecake. She

concentrated on swirling her fork in the glazed topping on the plate to avoid looking at Jacques. The last thing she wanted to talk about was New Orleans and the reason she had left the city and him. "When I first moved here, I got a job soliciting money for a charitable organization. I was pretty good at it. Then later when I had to take time off for the—"

Her stomach pitched when she realized just how much she had come close to revealing. Liza put down her fork and brought her hand to her lap to hide her trembling fingers. "Later, Peter suggested I try selling my services as a fund-raiser to other companies and organizations. Last year when he and Aimee came up with The Art For Kids' Sake project, he hired me as its fund-raiser."

"Neither he nor Aimee ever told me you were here." Something dark and angry shimmered in his eyes. "They claimed not to know where you were."

"They didn't—not at first. When they found out I was here I asked them not to tell you."

"Why?" Jacques demanded, his voice hard with emotion and making his accent more pronounced.

"Because it was time for us to move on. We wanted different things," she reminded him, remembering how shattered she had been that last night when she had finally accepted that they could never have any future together. That she could never share with him the wonderful gift he had given her.

"Yes. I remember. Where you are concerned, there is little I do not remember. For instance, I remember that last time we were together you told me you loved me. You even talked about marriage, children."

"And you made it clear that you weren't interested in any of those things." Jacques's rejection had crushed her. Not even her ex-husband's betrayal and the dissolution of her marriage had shattered her so badly. Even three years later, the memory still hurt.

"Is that why you left, *chérie?* Is it because I did not offer to marry you?"

"No. That's not why I left. You were always honest with me, Jacques. I knew from the beginning that you weren't in love with me and that you weren't interested in anything permanent like marriage."

"I cared for you, Liza. I still do." He caught her hand, brought it to his lips.

All the old feelings came back to her in a rush, making her remember what it had been like to be in his arms, making her want to be there again, making her wish she could tell him the truth.

"What we had was very special. We can have that again. I will be here until Christmas. We can—"

"Do what, Jacques? Resume our affair?"

What looked like regret flickered in his eyes, sending any hope she'd been harboring to a swift death. Liza pulled her hand free.

"I explained to you my reasons for vowing never to marry. I had hoped you would understand. You would have my affection and my fidelity. I have nothing more in me to give."

"Because you believe all those horrid lies your father told you," she tossed back. Anger ripped through her at the thought of the man who had poisoned his son's mind and heart. "You still believe you carry some sort of dark gene inside you and that makes you afraid to love anyone."

The warmth in his eyes dissolved, reminding Liza of those winter days when not even the sun could penetrate the bitter cold that blanketed the city. He leaned forward, his voice dropped to a whisper. "Believe me, Liza, such darkness does exist. I have seen firsthand the pain it can cause. While I want you, as I have never wanted another,

I refuse to risk passing that darkness inside me on to another—not even for you.''

Liza wanted to scream. She remained silent instead and buried any second thoughts she had been having about telling Jacques the truth. He would hate her and himself if he were to learn the real reason she had left him, the reason she had to walk away from him now. ''But that's not the reason we're here, is it? We're here to decide on the menu. Do you have any preference on the dessert?''

Jacques sighed and leaned back in his seat. ''The cheesecake.''

''I agree. I'll let Mr. Newberry know what we've decided on.'' Liza stood, eager to get away and regain the emotional ground she had lost. ''And I'd appreciate it if you would make some suggestions on what wines to serve. Mr. Newberry can let you know what type of budget we have to work with.''

''Liza, wait.''

''I really do have to get back to my office, Jacques.''

''Then I will take you,'' he said determinedly.

She started to argue, but didn't bother when she saw that stubborn set of his jaw. Too emotionally drained to argue further, she allowed him to steer her to the catering office to finalize the arrangements.

Forty-five minutes later when they exited the hotel's restaurant, Liza welcomed the sting of cold air that greeted her. She handed the valet the ticket for her car, then turned to face Jacques. ''Thanks for your input with the menu and the suggestions on the wine,'' she said, eager to keep things on a business footing.

''We both know that you did not need my help with the menu and it is not the reason I came.'' He smiled. ''You are.''

Liza's heart did a flutter kick and she glanced away from the devilish grin. ''All the same I appreciate your help,'' she managed to say coolly while silently chiding the valet for taking so long with her car.

Jacques fingered the lapels of her wool coat, pulling up the collar. He caressed her cheek with his finger, forcing her to face him. "Stop fighting me, Liza. Stop fighting yourself. Why not enjoy each other while we can?"

"I can't."

"Why not?"

Liza looked up into his eyes. "Because...because there's someone else."

Four

"I do not believe you," Jacques said, his voice hard. "You are not in love with Carstairs."

"No, I'm not. But it's not Robert I was referring to. It's...it's someone else."

Jealousy clawed at him, making him feel as though he couldn't breathe. "Who?" he demanded, grabbing her arm. Liza looked down at the fingers circling her arm, and Jacques released her at once, appalled by his actions. "Tell me his name."

"You...you don't know him."

Jacques narrowed his eyes, noting the slight tremor in her fingers as she continued to clench and unclench the strap of her purse and the way she refused to meet his gaze. He'd never known Liza to fidget. That unflappable calm of hers was as much a part of her as her blond beauty. In all the time he'd known her, only twice had she shown any signs of anxiety—the night she had decided they would become lovers and the last night they were together. In both instances she had been nervous about something, holding something back.

She was holding something back now. He was sure of it. She was every bit as tense now as she'd been that last night before she'd left him. Why? Jacques wondered. He'd known Liza had secrets and had sensed from the beginning that she'd been running from something in her past. Since he had spent a lifetime trying to escape from his own dark secrets, he'd never pressed her for details. Perhaps he should have. Perhaps he still should.

The valet driver pulled up to the curb and hopped out of the car. After tipping him, Jacques opened the door for Liza. Silence stretched between them as he watched her slide onto her seat and strap herself in with the seat belt. With his arms resting on the open door and roof of the car, he leaned down to look at her face.

"Goodbye, Jacques," she said, obviously waiting for him to move so she could close the door.

He didn't budge. "Things are not over between us, Liza. You and I both know that."

"I told you, there's someone else."

"And I told you, I do not believe you."

"Then that's your problem. Not mine. Now, if you don't mind, I want to leave." She tipped up her chin haughtily and stared straight ahead.

"Ah, but I do mind, *chérie*. I mind very much. *If* there is another man, he is no more your lover than Carstairs is."

"And how would you know that?" she demanded.

Jacques grinned, which, judging from the tightening of her lips, only angered her more. "I know because nothing has changed between you and me. If there were another man, you would not still want me. And you do want me, Liza, just as I want you." He brought his face closer to hers, watched the awareness register in her eyes. "Nothing can change the fact that the fire is still there between us.

Accept it, Liza. I have. Do not deny us this second chance that fate has offered us.''

Jacques started to kiss her, but Liza whipped her head to the side, causing his lips to feather her hair instead of her mouth. ''Fate had nothing to do with our meeting each other again and you know it. This is all Aimee's doing.''

''Fate takes many forms,'' Jacques informed her. ''You and I were destined to be lovers, Liza. We *will* be lovers again. You only lie to yourself if you think otherwise.''

Her fingers tightened on the steering wheel. ''I'm amazed that you can get your head through the door with that ego of yours.''

Jacques eased back and sighed. ''It is not ego, *ma chérie*. I am simply stating what we both know is true.''

''And I hate to burst that bubble of yours, Jacques. But you're deluding yourself. I told you, there's someone else.''

''Then who is he?''

''You don't know him,'' she said, her voice filled with exasperation.

''Is it that I do not know him? Or is it that he does not exist?''

She looked up at him then. Her eyes were dark with an emotion he couldn't identify, with a vulnerability he had only caught glimpses of in the past. ''Oh, he exists, all right.'' A bittersweet smile curved her lips. ''He's very real. You can take my word for it.''

But he wouldn't take her word for it, Jacques decided as he stepped back and watched Liza drive away. She was lying, he told himself, biting back the niggling doubt that had begun to gnaw its way into his consciousness, when he'd heard the conviction in her voice. She had to be lying. He had known enough women to recognize the difference between a response that was genuine and one that was fake. And Liza's response to him when they had kissed, the desire he had seen in her eyes, had been very real indeed. He was sure of it. He could feel it in his gut.

No, there was no other man. He had known that first time they had made love that no other man had tapped the passion in her that she kept so well hidden—not even her ex-husband. Just as there had never been any other woman who could make him feel as Liza did.

Liza was wrong if she thought things were over between them. They weren't. The two of them *would* be lovers again, Jacques promised himself as he watched the taillights of her car wink before she exited the building. It was fate.

Fate.

Jacques considered the word and the impact that it had had on his life. Retrieving the ticket for his rental car from his pocket, he made his way to the valet. He handed the stub to the young man. Frowning, Jacques considered Liza's response to his statement about fate. Perhaps Liza didn't believe in fate, but he certainly did. After all, it had been fate that had cursed him to be born with Gaston blood in his veins. And it had been the knowledge of the darkness that flowed through him that had made him vow to end the curse with himself.

It had been fate that had given Liza to him once and it had been fate that had brought her to him again. And she *would* be his again—at least for a while. And when they parted again, he would finally know peace. There would be no more sleepless nights lying awake hungering for a cool blonde with green eyes that sparkled and skin that smelled like gardenias. When they parted next time, he would be free.

"In addition to the centerpieces, I thought we could sprinkle some of these little red and green confetti Christmas trees along the center of the table," Liza explained to the florist. She held up the packages of metallic confetti cutouts that she had found in a craft store.

"Good idea. These will pick up the colors in the floral arrangements and add to the festive tone of the room." The other woman made a notation in her book. "Now what about the Christmas tree? Is there a particular kind you prefer? Frazier fir? Blue spruce? Scotch pine—"

"The biggest one you can find."

Liza stiffened at the sound of Jacques's voice. A shiver of awareness tripped down her spine as he walked across the room and joined her at the conference room table.

"If memory serves me correctly, Ms. O'Malley likes the tip of the tree to touch the ceiling," Jacques announced to the florist.

Liza swallowed at his reference to the first and only Christmas that they had shared together and her insistence that they purchase a tree that had been far too large for her small apartment. But it had been a magical time, a time for miracles, for new beginnings. She had been wildly in love with Jacques. During those months they were together, he had helped to free her from the sense of failure that had plagued her since her divorce. He had made her feel like a woman again. And although he hadn't given her his love as she'd hoped, he had given her something far more precious. A miracle that she had never thought to know.

"Well, I'm not sure about touching the ceiling," Emily Robbins, the owner of Emily's Flower Gardens said. "But I did get in several large blue spruces that might come close."

Liza pulled herself back to the present. "Actually, the hotel's already agreed to provide a Christmas tree for the ballroom, Emily. So we won't need to worry about one for the gala." Offering a smile that she knew was far too stiff, Liza turned to greet Jacques. "Jacques, this is Emily Robbins, the proprietor of Emily's Flower Gardens. She's handling the floral arrangements for the gala. Emily, this is Jacques Gaston, one of the committee's co-directors."

In typical Jacques fashion, he kissed Emily's hand. "My pleasure, Mademoiselle Robbins. Sorry I am late for our meeting," he told the florist. "Evidently I failed to make a note about the change of place and went to your shop by mistake. Your lovely assistant reminded me we were meeting here at Liza's office.''

Liza caught the mocking note in his voice. He knew darn well there had been no mistake. She hadn't bothered to notify him until the last minute about the change on this meeting or the other two appointments that she had rescheduled. As a result, she had successfully avoided seeing or speaking with Jacques for more than a week.

Evidently, her luck had just run out.

"Oh it's no problem," Emily Robbins replied. "And please, call me Emily."

Liza narrowed her eyes at the sudden warmth in the other woman's voice. What had happened to the tough-as-nails businesswoman she had been negotiating with on prices for the past several months? While the woman hadn't been cold, she hadn't been exactly friendly. Judging by the look on Emily Robbins's face at the moment, the thirty-something, no-nonsense entrepreneur had just fallen victim to the Jacques Gaston charm.

"Would you like me to go over the selections that Liza and I have already made?"

"That won't be necessary," Liza informed the florist, slightly miffed by the offer. "I'll bring Mr. Gaston up to speed on our meeting at another time."

"But I really don't mind."

"I'm sure you don't. But as I said, it isn't necessary."

"Liza is right," Jacques told the florist, favoring her with another of his engaging smiles. "I have complete faith in you two lovely ladies. I am sure whatever you and Liza have decided will be perfect."

Liza bit back her irritation at the other woman's beaming expression. "I know how busy you are, Emily, so I won't take up any more of your time. Thanks again for agreeing to meet me here on such short notice."

"No problem," Emily told her, obviously having difficulty keeping her eyes off Jacques.

Not that Liza could blame her. In his black sweater and dark slacks, his eyes looked like polished amber. His too long hair reminded her of wheat that she had once glimpsed in a field. The added combination of his French accent and lethal charm, made Jacques Gaston a difficult man to ignore.

As though sensing her scrutiny, Jacques shifted his gaze to her. Liza flushed, chastising herself for being caught staring at him. "Emily," she said, refusing to meet Jacques's eyes. "How soon before you can get back to me with the new total for the floral decorations?"

With obvious reluctance, Emily dragged her attention back to Liza. "I'll need to reconfirm with my suppliers on the price of the poinsettias and garland, then tally everything with the other changes we made. Is Monday morning soon enough?"

"Monday morning's fine."

"Good. I'll call you on Monday, then, and if everything's in order, I'll drop off the contract for you to sign that afternoon."

"Great." Liza nodded. "I'll talk to you next week."

"In the meantime, if you have any questions, Mr. Gaston—Jacques," she corrected at the arch of his brow, "please give me a call."

"I'll do that," Jacques said, a wicked smile curving his lips as he took the card Emily offered him.

Liza slapped her planning folder closed. "Well, I guess that's it. I'm afraid you'll both have to excuse me. I have another appointment due here in a few minutes."

"Of course," Emily replied, looking like a kitten with a fresh bowl of cream as she smiled back at Jacques, and the two of them started towards the door.

Liza turned her back on the retreating couple. Typical Jacques Gaston behavior. The man could charm a snake out of its skin. But it was more than his charm that had snared her all those years ago, Liza admitted. True, there had always been an aura of the forbidden about Jacques that had excited her and frightened her at the same time. But beneath that rakish charm and quick-as-a-trigger temper, there had been so much more to him than the devil-may-care gigolo he pretended to be. There had been a kindness and sensitivity in him, a genuine joy of life that had drawn her to him. And it had been his fierce determination not to become a victim of commitment or any deeper emotions that had driven her away.

Her chest tightened and Liza pushed the sad memories aside. She had no reason to feel sorry for herself. She had done what she'd had to do. Jacques had made his choice and she had made hers. She certainly had no right to feel jealous, she told herself, as Jacques chatted with Emily at the door. But jealousy was just what she did feel, Liza admitted when she heard Emily laugh at something Jacques said.

Irritated with herself, she forced herself to concentrate on the task at hand—putting away her notes and samples. When she heard the click of the door moments later and the soft tread of Jacques's footsteps as he came up behind her, she snatched up the file marked decorations. Retrieving the ribbon samples and pictures of floral arrangements scattered on the table, she began stuffing them into the expanding file.

"It is not going to work, *chérie*."

"What isn't going to work?" she asked. Gathering up the files, she walked across the room to her desk, feigning a nonchalance she was far from feeling.

"Trying to avoid me."

"And what makes you think I'm trying to avoid you?"

He sat on the edge of her desk and picked up the silver-framed photo. Liza's heart stopped for long seconds as he studied the face of the blond-haired boy with golden eyes.

"Probably the fact that the last three meetings on the agenda were rescheduled and yet you did not bother to inform me," he told her, returning the frame to the desk.

"I did inform you," she replied as her heart remembered how to beat again. "I left a message for you on the answering machine at Peter and Aimee's apartment telling you about the changes."

"Ah, yes. Those messages on the answering machine. All conveniently left at the apartment instead of at the gallery where you knew I would be, insuring that I would not learn of the changes until it was too late. Fortunately, I figured out your little game. Otherwise, I would have missed today's meeting as well."

"Are you accusing me of changing the meetings deliberately just so you would miss them?"

"Yes, I am."

"And why would I do a thing like that?" she demanded, chagrined that her ploy had been so transparent.

He shot her that mischievous grin. "It is obvious, *chérie*. You do not trust yourself to be with me."

"Honestly, Jacques. That ego of yours has really gone to your head." Pulling out the desk file for her next meeting, she shoved the drawer closed. "For your information, I am not afraid to be with you. I'm simply not interested."

"No?"

"No," she said firmly. "Believe it or not, those meetings were changed due to scheduling conflicts and had nothing to do with you whatsoever."

"Then you are saying that you are *not* afraid of what will happen between us while we are working together on this fund-raiser?"

"No. I am not afraid of what will happen between us, because nothing is going to happen."

He arched one brow in challenge.

Liza slapped her folder down on the desk and planted her hands beside it. She leaned forward. "Take my word for it, Jacques. Absolutely nothing is going to happen between us.''

''You are sure?''

''Positive.''

''Then it should not be a problem for you to attend a small dinner party I am having.''

Sighing, Liza straightened and picked up her file. ''Just because I'm not afraid of being with you, doesn't mean I'm interested in anything more than a business relationship. I'm not.'' She saw no point in reminding him again that there was someone else—especially considering the problem she would incur if she were forced to present that someone.

Jacques shook his head and made a reproving sound. ''So suspicious.''

''Can you blame me?'' she countered. ''Especially after that statement you made about…about…''

''About seducing you?'' He laughed. ''Oh, I still fully intend to seduce you, *chérie*. Make no mistake about that.''

Liza's traitorous pulse leapt at the promise in his voice, the flicker of heat in his eyes.

''But the dinner party is not part of that plan. It is actually business.''

Liza narrowed her eyes.

''It is true. I am holding a small party to announce the donation of one of my works for the gala's silent auction. You can check with Peter if you do not believe me.''

It took a moment for the meaning of his statement to register. Then shock set in. She knew from Peter that Jacques's paintings and sculptures had skyrocketed in value during the past few years. Several of his works were now commanding sums in the high five-figure range.

''Nothing to say? Do not tell me you are speechless. I have never known Liza O'Malley to be at a loss for words. That sharp tongue of yours was always one of the things I enjoyed most about you.'' There was laughter in his voice and the smile he gave her was pure sin. "But I have several very pleasant memories of finding ways to silence it."

Liza flushed, recalling vividly the many times he had silenced her with his own mouth.

"Well? What do you think?"

"I think it's incredibly generous of you. You would really be willing to donate one of your pieces for the auction?"

"Not only will I donate it, I will allow you to select the piece," he told her. "Choose from anything in Peter's gallery. That is, anything except *La Femme*," he said, his eyes darkening with desire. He reached out and drew his fingertip down her cheek. "It is the one piece I will never part with."

Liza's heart stammered. The familiar flutter of excitement began in her stomach and worked its way lower. Suddenly nervous, she drew back from his touch. "Thank you," she managed to say, only to be appalled by the husky tone of her voice. She swallowed. "Everyone will be thrilled, Jacques. This is really most generous of you. Just the money we raise from your gift alone will be enough to ensure the art camp for the kids will be a reality this summer."

"So you will come to my dinner party?"

"Yes. Of course. Just tell me when and where."

"Tomorrow night. Seven o'clock. At the Gallaghers' apartment."

"Tomorrow night?" she repeated, frowning.

"Yes. Is that a problem?"

"Uh, no. No problem." Liza hesitated, disliking the thought of being away from home in the evening, but realizing she would have to do so this time. It also meant she would have to make arrangements quickly and pray that Mrs. Murphy would be available on such short notice.

"I thought it would be best to make the announcement as soon as possible so that you will be able to advertise it before the gala itself. But I will delay the party if you wish.''

''No. Tomorrow night will be fine.''

He eased off the edge of the desk and moved around the desk to stand in front of her. ''You are sure?''

''Yes,'' Liza assured him. Under his questioning gaze, she felt more of an explanation for her hesitation was needed. ''It's just that I live outside the city as I mentioned before and I...well, I try to avoid driving at night whenever I can.''

''You are welcome to spend the night at the apartment,'' Jacques said with that devilish grin on his face.

''Thanks, but I think I'll pass.''

He moved a step closer, his body mere inches from her own. ''Are you sure I cannot change your mind?''

''Quite sure,'' she told him, her heart thudding in her chest.

At the knock on her door, Jacques hesitated and then stepped back. ''Tomorrow night, then.''

''Tomorrow night,'' she promised. As she watched him leave and her next appointment entered the office, Liza prayed that the next four weeks would go by quickly because she was finding it more and more difficult to say no to Jacques Gaston.

''I'm looking forward to that auction, Jacques, and you can count on me being the lady who's going to walk away with that sculpture.''

''It will give me great pleasure to see you do just that, Madame Davis.'' Jacques kissed the woman's hand and reminded himself to send Peter's assistant roses for suggesting that the monied art patron be included on his VIP guest list for tonight's dinner party.

After shaking several more hands, he closed the door on the last of the dinner guests. Finally everyone was gone except Liza. Anticipation raced through him like a champion stallion out of the starting gate. He forced himself to take a deep breath. From the moment she had walked into the apartment tonight, looking both cool and sexy in her winter white cocktail suit, his body had gone on full alert. He had wanted nothing more than to take her into his arms and kiss her until she was all ruffled and that polite look on her face had been replaced by one of desire. It had taken every ounce of control he possessed not to tell everyone to leave at once, that the party was over before it even began. Never in his life had he ever wanted a woman so badly as he wanted Liza O'Malley—not even three years ago when *she* had been the woman he had wanted.

Three weeks ago he had told himself it was part vengeance, part desire that had made him pursue her. Now he was no longer so sure. One thing he did know was that he would never experience peace again until Liza was his once more. He still wanted her with a passion that bordered on obsession. And despite her denials and silly fabrication of another lover, he knew that she still wanted him.

Pushing away from the door, Jacques went in search of Liza. He found her in the kitchen, stacking the last of the wineglasses into the dishwasher.

A makeshift apron was wrapped around her waist, pulling up the edge of her hem slightly on one side. Jacques smiled. His gaze skimmed the length of those legs appreciatively and then moved up and across the ivory skirt that covered that sweet little bottom of hers.

He was still contemplating her bottom and the fact that her hips were slightly fuller now than they had been three years ago, when Liza turned to place another glass in the dishwasher. Spotting him, she jumped. The glass slipped from her fingers and she shrieked as it fell to the floor and shattered. "Oh God, Jacques, I'm sorry," she said, stooping down to pick up the broken glass. "I didn't hear you come in over the music and when I turned around and saw you—"

"Forget about it. It is only a glass." He stooped down beside her.

"It's Aimee's good crystal."

"I will replace it," he insisted, taking the broken shards from her hand.

Liza left him to retrieve the broom and dustpan. "Jacques, be careful or you'll cut—"

The jagged stem sliced through his thumb. Reverting to his native French, Jacques cursed at the sudden sting and the sight of blood spilling forth. He dumped the pieces of glass into the trash bin.

"Look what you've done," Liza admonished.

"I assure you it was not deliberate."

"You should have been more careful." She pulled him over to the sink and stuck his hand under the faucet. "Stay there," she commanded and disappeared from the room.

Seconds later she was back with a box of bandages and antiseptic. Turning off the water, she dried the cut and applied pressure to stop the bleeding.

"It is only a scratch," Jacques informed her. He slid his free arm around her waist to draw her closer and steal a kiss—a kiss he had been wanting all evening. God, but she smelled good.

"Behave yourself." She shot him that cool duchess look while continuing to minister to his hand. "It's definitely more than a scratch, but you're right. It doesn't look too deep." She swatted at his arm until he released her, then retrieved the small brown bottle and box of Band-Aids. "I'm going to put some antiseptic and a bandage on it just the same. You don't want any infection to set in."

Leaning against the counter, Jacques grinned at Liza. "While I admit to wanting to feel your hands on my body, *chérie*, this is not what I had in mind."

Awareness.

He watched it register in Liza's eyes before she had a chance to bank it. Despite the nasty slice on his thumb, he was keenly aware of her light floral scent, the feel of her soft fingers on him, the nearness of her body. He had waited all evening to be alone with her, to taste that soft mouth again. He could almost feel the hot, sweet tightness wrapping itself around him.

Jacques sucked in his breath, his fantasy bubble bursting at the sudden sting.

"Be still," Liza ordered, as she painted his thumb with another coat of antiseptic. "There. That should do it." After quickly slapping on the bandage, she started to move away.

Jacques caught her hand. "Not so fast, Florence Nightingale." He rubbed his thumb lazily across the inside of her wrist and smiled at the sudden quickening of her pulse. He leaned a fraction closer, bringing his mouth mere inches from hers.

"You should be returning to your other guests," Liza informed him.

"Everyone else has already gone."

Her eyes widened before she replied. "Then I should be going, too." She unfastened her apron and took a step back.

Jacques smiled as she met the edge of the kitchen counter. With the kitchen sink to her right, the island stove to her left and him in front of her, Liza had little room to escape. "Aren't you going to kiss me to make sure I do not have a fever?"

"I doubt that a simple little cut like that would cause you to run a fever."

"But you cannot be certain. Even as we speak, some terrible infection could be racing through my bloodstream. Why not kiss me and find out?"

A smile tugged at the corner of her lips. "You don't give up, do you, Gaston?"

"Not when it is something I want. And I very much want you to kiss me, Liza."

The laughter faded from her lips. "If I'm checking for

temperature, it's supposed to be your brow that I kiss, not your mouth.''

"As usual, you Americans have it all wrong." He caught her hand and drew her toward him. Heat spread through him and he bit back a groan as her soft, warm body pressed against him.

He caught the hitch in her breath. Her eyes shot up to meet his as the evidence of his arousal thrust against her. Unable to resist, Jacques lowered his head. Gently he brushed his mouth back and forth, outlined the shape of her lips with his tongue. "Liza," he whispered her name.

She hesitated, but he continued to brush soft kisses across her mouth, stroking the seam of her lips with his tongue. Finally she sighed and he slipped his tongue inside to find hers. As she touched her tongue to his, Jacques admitted that no other woman had ever felt this right in his arms. Something shifted inside him, prodding that empty place where he knew his heart should have been. Only with Liza had it ever been like this. So hot. So demanding. So free.

And then suddenly he was beyond thinking, beyond reasoning. All he could do was feel as she tempted and teased him with her mouth. She clung to his shoulders, shaped her body to his. When she arched herself against him and deepened the kiss, Jacques thought he would go mad.

He gripped her hips, lifted her to the counter. Pushing up her skirt, he ran his fingers up over her knees, along her stockinged legs, across the lace tops of her hose to the inside of her bare thighs. He devoured her mouth, thrusting his tongue inside to mate with hers while he spread her legs wider. He cupped the heat at her center.

"Jacques," Liza cried out as he imitated the movement with his finger through the silk of her panties.

Her breath whispered along his neck, sending rivulets of pleasure through him as he felt her grow wet and hot and ready for him, dampening his fingers through the silk of her panties. His breath was coming faster. His shaft strained against the fly of his slacks. Suddenly he didn't think he could wait for her a moment longer. "Ah, *chérie*. It has been so long. I have wanted you so much. We will go to the bedroom later. I do not think I can wait that long to be inside you." He reached for the edge of her panties to slip his fingers into her moist heat and prepare her for him.

"Wait! Jacques, no. Wait!"

He struggled to slow his breathing at the panic in her voice. His gaze shot up to Liza's face. Jacques went still at her stricken expression. "What is it? What is wrong, Liza?"

"This is a mistake," she said, shoving down her skirt. She scrambled off the counter and covered her face with her hands. After taking several deep breaths, she dropped her hands and met his gaze. The eyes that looked at him were still glazed with passion. But there was also confusion, regret.

It was the regret that had him clenching his jaw, balling his hands into fists at his sides.

"I'm sorry, Jacques. This is my fault. I never should have let this happen. I never should have allowed things to go this far. I guess there's no point in denying that I'm still attracted to you."

"Attracted?" he repeated, the word an angry hiss. He saw no point in hiding his irritation.

Her lips tightened a fraction. "All right. I admit it. I want you. Satisfied?"

"No, Liza. I am *definitely* not satisfied." Biting back his frustration and the painful ache in his groin, Jacques continued, "My only consolation is that I know you are not satisfied, either."

"I'm sorry, Jacques. Truly I am. But I can't let this happen." Turning on her heel, she started toward the living room.

"Why?" Jacques demanded as he followed her, his anger increasing with each step. When she retrieved her coat from the closet, his patience snapped. He caught her chin, forced her to look at him. "Why, Liza? And do not lie to me and tell me there is another man. I do not believe you—not when you go up like flames in my arms. In another five minutes, I could have had you on top of the kitchen counter. You and I both know it."

When she didn't argue the point, he continued, "You have said yourself that you want me. I have already told you that I want you. So why are you denying us the pleasure we can give one another?"

Liza jerked herself free. "Because it's not enough," she told him. "It's just not enough."

"What is it you want?"

"More than you're willing to give." She pulled on her coat.

"Meaning what?"

"Meaning that in another three weeks the gala will be over and then you'll be gone. You'll go back to your life and I'll go back to mine. I was foolish to engage in a casual affair with you three years ago. I have no intention of doing so again."

"I assure you, no affair between us was or will ever be casual."

She tipped up her chin, gave him that haughty "duchess to peasant" look that she did so well. "And I assure you, it's a moot point. Because there isn't going to be any affair."

"Ah, but you are wrong, *chérie,*" Jacques said to her retreating back. If anything, he was more determined than ever to make her his again.

Five

The man was driving her crazy.

Liza threw her pencil down on the desk and glared at the fragrant gardenias with their lush green leaves that had arrived that morning nestled in a gold-painted basket. Picking up the note that had accompanied them, she reread the ridiculous verse scrawled in Jacques's bold hand.

On the eighth day of Christmas, your lover gives to you, eight white gardenias....
Do you remember, *chérie?* It can be that way again—
Jacques.

How could she not remember the afternoon he had made love to her on a bed strewn with gardenia petals? The scent had wrapped itself around her, around them, making their coming together even more erotic, more special.

Why was he doing this? she demanded in silent frustration. Why was he going to such pains to make sure she remembered every detail of their affair?

Liza sighed. Of course, she knew the answer to that one—he wanted her. And he obviously had every intention of keeping his promise to seduce her. Flustered, Liza crumpled the note in her hand. And after that disastrous evening of the party when she had come so close to giving into her desire for him, he had every reason to believe that he would succeed.

And you have no one to blame for that but yourself, Liza O'Malley.

It was true, she admitted, pressing her fingers to her burning cheeks as she recalled how dangerously close she had come to making love with him that night. She had brought Jacques's relentless pursuit upon herself by allowing things to progress as far as they had that evening. There had been no question that she had welcomed his advances, had even wanted them. Pulling back when she did had been inexcusable, especially given her response to him. The extent of his anger had been proof of that. Liza's throat went dry as she remembered the fury in his eyes, the muscle ticking in his cheek, the clipped note in his voice as he spoke to her.

When more than a week had passed without him calling her or showing up at any of the other gala meetings, she had assumed he had decided getting her into his bed wasn't worth the effort. That he had washed his hands of her.

And then the gifts had started.

The first one had arrived eight days ago—twelve days before the gala patron party—a bottle of champagne from the Gaston vineyards in France. She had known without looking at the card that it had come from Jacques.

Two crystal champagne flutes had arrived the second day, followed by three silver bowls of strawberries. The four fortune cookies with their specially worded fortunes predicting old lovers would reunite had put her on full alert.

Each gift had been carefully chosen to trigger memories of their affair in New Orleans—including today's gardenias.

Pain ripped through her at the memory of the last time Jacques had given her gardenias, that last night they were together in New Orleans. Even after all this time, the memory was as fresh as if it had only been yesterday....

"I love you," Liza had whispered as she'd snuggled in Jacques's embrace. "I don't think I've ever been happier in my entire life than I am right now...at this moment...being with you."

"Ah, and you are not the only one who is happy." He kissed her again, deeply, soundly. "You are so beautiful, so responsive, *ma chérie,*" Jacques murmured against her lips. He slid one leg between hers, and she could feel his hardness nudging against her.

"Sometimes I think you are a witch who has cast a spell over me," he continued, his eyes darkening to amber as he looked down at her. "No matter how often I make love to you, it is not enough. Sometimes I fear I will never be able to get enough of you." As though to prove his point, he shoved aside the sheet. His fingers glided over her bare hip to tangle in the curls between her thighs.

Liza's breath snagged in her throat as he stroked the mouth of her sex with his finger. Already she could feel the heat pooling deep inside her, making her want him again. She looked into the face of the golden Adonis she had given her heart and her body to. Cupping his face between her hands, she pulled him to her and kissed him with all the love in her soul. "Would it be so bad?" she asked, when he ended the kiss. "I mean, if things didn't end between us? If we continued to want each other...decided to stay together?"

Jacques narrowed his eyes, and though he didn't move, Liza sensed his withdrawal. "It would be a disaster—for both of us."

"Why?"

"Because I have told you, I do not want any roots. Besides, I cannot stay in New Orleans forever. I have already stayed much longer than I had planned to, probably longer than it was wise to. But I have not wished to leave you."

"Then don't. Stay with me. I want you to stay."

He caught her fingers, brought them to his lips. "For a little longer, but then I must go. We both must get on with our lives."

"I want a life with you, Jacques."

"There is no place in my life for anyone, Liza. Not even you. Besides, what of your plans to travel? What of your plans to open your own business?"

"I could still do those things."

"But would you? Would you be willing to take a job in say, California, if my work kept me here? Or would you close down your business to fly with me to Milan or expect me to pass on Milan and stay with you?"

"We could compromise."

Jacques shook his head. "And then our passion for one another would turn to hate for being forced to give up our dreams." He kissed her. There was a sadness in his eyes, a longing that went deeper than physical desire. If only he would trust her, trust her love for him. "No, my Liza. You and I are alike in that respect. We are selfish in that we both know what we want and are not afraid to go after it. And right now what I want is you."

Tell him, a voice inside her whispered. Tell him. "Jacques, I..." She hesitated, suddenly unsure. When he reached for her again, Liza held him at bay.

"What is it, *ma chérie?*"

"I...I've been thinking a lot about the future. Have you ever thought about the future?"

"Of course I think of the future. What artist does not? Someday I will be famous, Liza. My art will be carried only in the top galleries. I will stay only in the finest hotels, eat at the best restaurants, drink the finest champagnes—even those produced in my father's vineyard," he finished, a touch of bitterness lacing his voice. His eyes grew stormy for a moment as he dragged his fingers through his hair.

"What is it, Jacques?"

He shook his head and seemed to shake off whatever had bothered him. Because when he looked at her again, he was the Jacques she knew. The man with big dreams and ambitions. He painted the scene for her as he had done often in the past. "Someday when I am famous and wealthy, I will make love to you in a grand suite of a luxury hotel. There will be fresh flowers everywhere in genuine crystal vases, carpets so lush your feet will sink to the ankle. There will be a big bed with silk sheets that glide across your skin. And when I lay you on that bed to make love to you, instead of a scattering of petals from a few stolen gardenias, the bed will be lined with the petals from a hundred gardenias from the best florist in town."

Liza's heart leapt in her chest—more at his reference to a future that included her than the erotic images his words created. "Those are just things, Jacques. They're not important to me."

"But they are important to me."

His answer was like an arrow to her heart. Still she refused to give up. Swallowing her pride, she asked, "After the fame, after the money, then what? What happens after?"

"What do you mean?"

"I mean, what will you do when you attain your dream? Do you...do you think you'll want to settle down? You know, get married. Have a family."

The smile in his eyes withered, and despite the warm temperatures, a chill chased down Liza's spine at the coldness that took its place. "I will never marry, Liza. And I will most definitely never have children."

Her throat suddenly dry, Liza swallowed. "But what

if...what if you fell in love with someone? Maybe even found out you were going to be a father?"

"It will not happen. I am always very careful of that."

"I know. But what if, despite your precautions, it happened anyway? What would you do?"

His eyes searched hers for long moments. Just when she was sure he wasn't going to answer, he said, "I would insist we get rid of it."

Liza flinched, unable to hide her shock. "You don't mean that."

"But I do," he insisted. His expression grew bitter, cold. "I will never be responsible for bringing a child into this world. The blood that runs through my veins is tainted. There is a darkness in me, a darkness that was in my father and his father before him. A darkness that has been passed on to me, but will end with me."

"Jacques, that's ridiculous," she told him, but she could see that he believed every word he said. She stroked his jaw. "There is no darkness in you. You're one of the kindest, most generous people I know. I love you."

He caught her fingers, kissed them. "You love the part of me that I have allowed you to see."

"I love you," she countered.

"Trust me, *chérie*. You would not love me—not the real Jacques Gaston, not the whole Jacques Gaston. How could you when even I despise who and what I am?"

When she started to argue, he silenced her with a look. "There is an ugliness, a darkness inside me that you have not seen, Liza, that you will never see if I can help it. But it is there just the same. I have seen it, felt it clawing inside me like a hungry beast demanding to be fed. It is there every time I get angry, every time I find myself growing jealous of the way other men look at you."

"I never knew you were jealous."

"Jealous is a mild term for what I feel when I see you near another man. When I heard that man ask you for your phone number at the party last night, I wanted to kill him with my bare hands. I would have, too, if you had given it to him." She could see the fire in his eyes and realized he meant every word. He trailed his fingers down her cheek, circled her throat. He pressed his thumb across her windpipe, causing her pulse to scatter. He looked at her, menace in his eyes. "Still, for a moment, I wanted to strangle you for smiling at him even though you refused."

Liza trembled despite her effort not to do so. She swallowed. "I suppose being jealous is only natural when you love someone," she offered.

Jacques laughed, but the sound held no mirth, no joy. "A man like me does not love, Liza. I am incapable of such a noble emotion. What I feel for you is passion."

Pressing Liza back onto the mattress, he captured the tip of her breast in his mouth, greedily taking the nipple between his teeth while covering her other breast with his hand. For the first time ever, Jacques's touch brought her no pleasure.

When he spread her legs apart and moved himself between them, Liza cried out, "Jacques, no."

Something dark and dangerous glittered in his eyes a moment, and she thought he was going to ignore her. Then he turned away from her. "I am sorry," he said, disgust in his voice. He placed an arm over his eyes. For endless minutes silence stretched between them. The only sound was the ticking of the clock and her own rapidly beating heart.

"Jacques, it's all right," she told him as she went to him and touched his shoulder.

But when he turned to face her again, his expression still held a trace of the anger and darkness she'd seen moments before. "Do not confuse lust with love, Liza. And be grateful that it is passion you inspire in me and not love. Because were I to let myself love you, I would cause you nothing but pain."

Caressing her face, Jacques cuddled her to him. But despite his nearness, Liza felt cold inside. Closing her eyes, she feigned sleep as he continued to stroke her hair gently. He murmured something in French to her, then said, "Rest now, *ma chérie*. Tomorrow will be a busy day for both of us with Peter's new exhibit opening." He kissed the top of her head. "And you and I will have much to celebrate after my first showing at Gallagher's."

But she hadn't been there to celebrate his success that next evening. Or any of the other successes that had followed. Because while Jacques had slept, she had returned to her own apartment, packed her bags and left.

And when she had boarded the flight out of New Orleans early the next morning, she had abandoned any hope she had of ever being a part of Jacques's life and any thoughts of ever telling him the truth.

Staring at the basket of gardenias, Liza pulled herself back from the fog of memories. She ran her fingertip over one delicate petal. Gardenias in December, she thought, shaking her head in wonder as she glanced from the spring blossoms to the snow falling outside. Only Jacques could present a gift that was a miracle unto itself.

But this offering in no way compared to the other precious gift, the other miracle he had given her. She had realized, the last night they'd been together, that he would never welcome the miracle he had helped to create.

But *she* had.

Liza hugged her arms to herself and thought of all those years of disappointment—the loss of her ovary, the temperature charts and fertility shots, the recurrence of the endometriosis and the doctor's recommendation that she consider a hysterectomy. She thought of the strain infertility had taken on her marriage, the discovery of her husband's affair, the pain and humiliation of the divorce so he could marry his pregnant girlfriend. Then after resigning herself to being little more than an empty shell of a woman, incapable of performing that most elemental function of the female body, she had become pregnant.

But in realizing one dream she had forsaken another—the dream that she and Jacques might share a life together. She had accepted that fact three years ago when she had made her decision to leave and not tell him he was going to be a father. And the one thing she had discovered in these past few weeks was that while Jacques might still want her physically, his heart remained closed, trapped by his fears of the past. If anything he was harder, more determined than ever not to allow himself to love. While she might risk his rejection of her, she would not risk his rejection of their child.

Picking up the basket of gardenias, she inhaled their sweet fragrance one last time, then dumped them into the trash bin beside her desk. Her chest tightened as she looked down at the crushed blooms. Curling her hands into fists at her side, she turned away to prevent herself from reaching down to save the broken flowers. For her son's sake, she had to be strong. She had to continue to resist Jacques despite her feelings for him. Only one more week, she told herself, and then he would be gone from her life for good.

"Liza?"

Liza swallowed, whipping back the sudden lump in her throat before turning around. "Yes, Mary. What is it?" she asked her assistant who stood at the door.

"The catering manager from the Knickerbocker, that Mr. Newberry, he's on the phone for you. He says it's important. Some sort of problem with the wine order for the benefit next weekend."

"Thanks. I'll take it."

She gave Liza a long look. "You okay?"

"I'm fine," she lied, returning to her desk. She reached for the phone. "Hello, Mr. Newberry. This is Liza O'Malley."

"Oh, Ms. O'Malley, I'm so glad I was able to reach you. I hope I haven't caught you at a bad time. Your assistant said you were about to leave for the day."

"No problem. What can I do for you?"

"As I was telling your assistant, I wanted to know how you would like me to handle the, um, problem about the difference in pricing on the wines."

Liza frowned, recalling the lunch meeting in which she had left the wine selections in Jacques's hands. Feeling a sudden pinch of guilt, she also remembered her eagerness to avoid further contact with Jacques and telling him he did not need to consult with her further on the decision. "Exactly what kind of pricing difference are we talking about?"

"Well, you'll remember when I initially quoted you on the wines, I recommended what I thought would be suitable vintages, a fine but moderately priced California Chablis and a Cabernet Sauvignon."

Liza pursed her lips as she picked up on the man's nervousness. She could all but see the man wiping his brow. "Yes, I remember. It was more than we had hoped to spend, but the committee's board did as you suggested and opted for the better wine instead of the house brands. I thought Mr. Gaston went over the selections with you and approved them."

"He did go over them, but he made substitutions."

"But within the same price range, right?"

"Not exactly."

Liza's stomach jerked. "Does that mean the wine cost even more than we originally estimated?"

"Yes, it did."

Biting back a groan, Liza chastised herself for not handling the wine selections herself. She knew how expensive Jacques's tastes were. Evidently he had opted for better wines than those suggested by Mr. Newberry, wines more expensive than they could afford. "How much more are we talking about, Mr. Newberry?'' she asked and immediately began to recalculate the margin of profit, wondering if cutting back on the balloons and floral decorations could make up for the additional costs.

"Four thousand dollars."

"All right. If we were to cut out the ice carving, that would save us another two hundred—" Liza stopped. Surely she hadn't heard him correctly. "How much did you say?"

"Four thousand dollars, give or take a few dollars."

"But that's impossible," she told him, shocked. "How can it be that much over, when our entire budget for the wine wasn't even that much?"

"I know it wasn't, Ms. O'Malley, and I explained that to Mr. Gaston when he insisted on ordering the French wines. But he said he would handle it and there wouldn't be a difference in pricing."

Liza narrowed her eyes. "He ordered French wines?"

"And champagne."

"What brand?" Liza asked.

"Gaston Vineyards Select."

Fury ripped through her. Liza tightened her fingers around the telephone receiver, wishing it were Jacques's neck. "Mr. Newberry, do you mean to tell me that when Mr. Gaston instructed you to change the wine order, when he told you to order wines that were more than twice what we had agreed we could afford, when he added champagne to that order as well, that you didn't think you should consult with me first before making those changes?"

"I wanted to, Ms. O'Malley. But Mr. Gaston assured me he had full authority to make the changes. Besides, he said he was related to the owners of Gaston Vineyards and assured me the wines would be discounted to reflect the prices we had agreed upon."

"I take it they weren't."

"No. We just received the shipment, and there's a copy

of the invoice with the order. I'm afraid that these prices don't even come close to those of the original wines we discussed.''

"Have you advised Mr. Gaston yet?"

"I've tried, but I haven't been able to reach him. I was told he left the gallery and I didn't have a residence number where I could reach him." He sighed. "What do you want me to do about the wine for the dinner? Even at our cost and just charging a corkage fee, the prices are going to be considerably higher than our original quote to you."

"We won't be serving Mr. Gaston's wines or his champagne, Mr. Newberry. Box them up for return."

"But what about the wines for the dinner?"

"Can you still get the ones we originally discussed?"

"I can get some, but I doubt that I can get the quantities we need that quickly. You'll remember, it's the Christmas season."

Which meant supplies were running low and deliveries even slower. "Do what you can and substitute where you have to."

"What about Mr. Gaston?"

"Don't worry about Mr. Gaston. I'll handle him."

And boy would she handle him, Liza thought ten minutes later as she stormed out of her office and headed for the Gallaghers' apartment.

"Come in," Jacques yelled over the strains of Mozart while continuing to smooth his thumb along what was the jawline of the clay sculpture.

The pounding sounded again, this time more in earnest. "I said it is open," he repeated. He looked from the photograph of Sarah Gallagher, Aimee and Peter's daughter, to the bust he was making of the child's head.

"Jacques?"

His pulse automatically beat faster at the sound of Liza's voice. "I'm in the studio," he called out. So the gardenias had done the trick, he thought, smiling as he heard the soft tapping of her heels on the floor. Ah, the language of flowers. While she had ignored his other gifts, she hadn't been able to resist the gardenias.

Lightly stroking his fingers along the cheek of the sculpture, he was still congratulating himself on locating the flowers in the dead of winter when the footsteps stopped at the doorway of the room. "Be right with you," he told her as he wet his thumb and gently pressed it at the curve of the figure's cheek to duplicate the dimple in the life-size version of the little girl. Satisfied, he turned to face Liza.

With her cheeks flushed and her blond hair lying in wind-tossed tangles around the shoulders of her open navy coat, she didn't look the least bit cool and proper now. She looked sexy as hell. He smiled. "Hello, *ma chérie*."

"You've gone too far this time, Jacques."

Jacques arched his brow, taken aback by the sharp note in her voice, the snapping fire in her green eyes. "You did not like the gardenias?"

"I'm not talking about the gardenias."

Puzzled, Jacques studied her more closely. No, while she did look sexy, she did not resemble in the least a woman who was enamored and on the verge of capitulating to his romantic gestures. "And I take it you are not talking about the silk scarves, either. No, you cannot be," he said more to himself than to her. "Those are not supposed to be delivered until the end of the week."

"Silk scarv— You didn't," she said, her eyes widening in astonishment or outrage, he wasn't sure which.

"Ah, but I did. Twelve of them—all made of silk—that I chose myself. You will receive them on Friday." He grinned as she opened her mouth and then closed it. "I take it you do remember our little game with the silk scarf," he prompted, referring to the erotic turn their love-making had taken when the scarf Liza had been wearing one day had been put to use as a instrument of pleasure.

Liza's cheeks turned a deeper shade of pink. Her back grew even more stiff. "I did not come here to discuss your...your foolish attempts to seduce me."

Her words smacked like a cuff to his chin, but he did his best to shake off his disappointment. Calmly he covered with a damp cloth the sculpture he had been working on and draped it with plastic before turning to face her again. "Then exactly why did you come here?"

"To tell you I know what you did. I know you changed the wine order for the fund-raiser."

"I am sorry you found out about it so soon," he said, disappointed that she had discovered the substitution early. He had hoped to have her discover his generous gift the night of the gala. "I was hoping to surprise you."

"You surprised me all right. How could you do such a thing, Jacques?"

Confused by her clipped tone, he repeated, "I told you I wanted to surprise you."

For some reason his answer only seemed to make her angry. "You knew we were on a tight budget. That we needed every penny we could raise for the summer camp. And while I can understand your wanting to help your family in France, I—"

"What is wrong with you, Liza? And what is this talk of me helping my family? I have no family in France or anywhere else." Frowning, Jacques picked up a towel and began to wipe the clay from his fingers. "I ordered the wine from Gaston Vineyards because *I* own Gaston Vineyards. I inherited it when my father died two years ago."

"Well, that makes it even worse," Liza told him, her voice as stiff as her spine. "That you would take advantage of the situation...of me like this."

Stunned by her accusation, Jacques could feel his own anger spark, shoot a burning path up his neck, to his cheeks. He threw down the towel and took a step toward her. "*Mon Dieu!* I give you one of my most expensive pieces of art for your auction. I make a fool of myself trying to romance you with gifts and love verses. I donate thousands of dollars of wine for your fund-raiser. All in an effort to please *you*. And yet you dare to stand there, look down your regal little nose at me and accuse me of taking advantage of you?''

"You…you donated the wine?"

"Of course I donated the wine," Jacques retorted. "You and your committee could not possibly afford wine from the Gaston Vineyards with that pitiful budget you gave Newberry to work with."

"But the copy of the invoice that came with the shipment. Mr. Newberry said…"

Jacques narrowed his eyes as understanding dawned. She thought he was attempting to line his pockets at the expense of the summer camp for kids. That he had used his position on the committee to make a few measly dollars for himself. Jacques gritted his teeth. "The invoice was for shipping purposes only. I have no intention of billing you or your committee for those wines. They are a gift from me."

Liza lowered her gaze. "I don't know what to say, Jacques. You were being generous and I thought—I thought—"

"It is obvious what you thought. I could understand Newberry making the mistake. But you, Liza? I thought you knew me better than that," he told her, disgusted that she had doubted his motives, surprisingly hurt that she had thought so little of him. He wanted to shake her for doubting him. He turned away from her instead.

"I'm sorry, Jacques. You're right. I should have realized there was a mistake. That you wouldn't be so…so mercenary."

Jacques swallowed the bitter taste his own anger had left in his mouth as her words washed over him, soothing his temper, his hurt. He had spent a lifetime learning to harness the beast of his temper and for the most part he succeeded. Except where Liza was concerned. Of all the people he had known in his life, only she stirred the emotions inside him so deeply, so quickly. Only she unleashed the anger, the jealousy, the need. Only she could tame his emotions so swiftly.

Do yourself a favor, Gaston. Forget about her. Forget about trying to seduce her.

But he couldn't forget her, Jacques admitted. He wanted her too much.

"I really am sorry, Jacques." She touched his shoulder. It was a gentle pressing of her fingers to convey her sincerity, but the action sent a jolt of awareness and longing through him. "I hope you'll forgive me for doubting you."

Silence hung suspended for long moments as he struggled to control the rush of hunger clawing at him. When he turned to face her, Jacques caught her hand before she could move away. "I will forgive you on one condition."

She eyed him warily. "What condition?"

"Come with me to the patron party on Friday night."

"I don't think—"

"For once, Liza, do not think. Just come with me," he urged her. He brought her fingers to his lips and kissed them lightly, when he wanted to do so much more. "Come with me. Please."

When she hesitated, he pressed on, adapting the persona he knew she would expect of him. "You Americans are famous for saying there is safety in numbers. Well, there will be at least fifty other people at the party. How much safer can you be?"

Six

There wasn't anything the least bit safe about being with Jacques Gaston, Liza decided. Regardless if there were an army of other people present, the man was just as dangerous, just as lethal to her emotionally as he had ever been.

The scarves had been waiting for her when she arrived at her office just after lunch on Friday. Twelve beautifully wrapped boxes from Neiman-Marcus, each containing a scarf made of the finest silk, each more beautiful, more exquisite than the next.

"Do you remember, Liza?" his note had read. *"That evening we skipped out on that boring party and went back to your apartment. You were wearing an ivory silk scarf..."*

A breath shuddered through her, and Liza pushed the memory aside. Of course she remembered, just as Jacques had intended she should. In fact, she had been able to think of little else the rest of the day.

And she had still been thinking about him when he had arrived at her office to pick her up for the party. In a dark gray suit that made his eyes look more golden than brown, his smile had been filled with sensual appreciation and promise as he brushed his lips against hers in greeting. It had taken every ounce of control she possessed not to respond to his kiss, to keep her expression cool when she felt anything but.

The close confines of the car hadn't helped. She had been far too conscious of Jacques's nearness, his scent, the way his fingers stroked the gearshift of the car as they made the drive to the Carstairs estate where the patron party was being held. Even now, despite the gay atmosphere and a room filled with people, she remained just as tense, her nerves wound just as tightly as a spring, simply because Jacques was in the same room.

"Can I get you a refill?"

Liza's head jerked up, and she stared at Robert Carstairs. She looked down at the nearly empty wineglass in her hand, then back up to him. "Thanks, but I think I'd better pass. I have a long drive home."

He quirked one brow in that manner she always associated with his aristocratic breeding. "Gaston isn't taking you home?"

She knew the question he was asking, the one he had been too polite to voice even when she had informed him weeks earlier that she could offer him nothing more than friendship. He'd expressed his disappointment and accepted her explanation that she simply wasn't ready for a serious relationship. But she had known then that he had wondered if it was because of Jacques. Evidently, given her friend Jane's questions, Robert wasn't the only one who was wondering if she and Jacques were lovers. "No, Jacques isn't taking me home and I won't be going back to his apartment. He picked me up at my office. I left my car there. We agreed that when the party's over, he'll take me back there and I'll drive myself home."

"I see." He paused. "I suspect that's your idea and not his."

Liza could feel the flush of color crawl up her cheeks. Of course, Robert was too perceptive not too notice Jacques's small statements of possessiveness where she was concerned. The hand at her elbow when they'd arrived, the innocent brush of his arm against hers, the familiarity implied by his taking a sip of wine from her glass. Given his earlier confession about being jealous, she had no doubt that the gestures had been warnings to Robert and anyone else that she belonged to him. Each spoke of an intimacy that went beyond being old acquaintances or business associates. It implied an intimacy shared by lovers. Ordinarily she would have been angered by Jacques's ploys, but her emotions had been too battered and weak to bother. "Yes. It was my idea."

Robert shifted his gaze to where Jacques stood in the midst of a circle of the guests. His lean face, with all its angles and planes and the slash of high cheekbones, was smiling at something being said, but his eyes were pinned on Liza. "I'm surprised he agreed."

"I'm afraid he didn't have much choice," Liza said, recalling just how unhappy Jacques had been at her insistence that she be picked up at the office and returned there when the party was over.

"Liza, I know this isn't the time or place, but if I'm wrong about you and Gaston... I mean if things aren't as serious between you two as I thought, I had hoped that you and I...that is, I had thought that we..." He took a deep breath. "I don't think friendship is such a bad place to start. I'm in no hurry. I'd give you as much time as you needed."

Liza took Robert's hand and squeezed it. She couldn't give him false hope. She knew she could never love him. He deserved a woman who would. "Robert, you're a wonderful man. Smart and kind and I'll always be very fond of you."

"But you're in love with Gaston."

"Yes." She sighed. "I'm sorry. More sorry than you can ever know."

"Don't be. I figured as much. But I had to give it a try." Giving her a wink, he smiled, then squeezed her fingertips once before releasing her hand. "What about our frowning Frenchman over there? How does he feel?"

"He wants me."

He chuckled. "Yes. I sort of figured that out myself, too. And I can't say that I blame him." Robert's grin spread. "But aside from the obvious, what else does he want? Has he said anything about the future?"

"Jacques isn't big on commitment. It's part of the reason things ended between us before."

"I see. Then, I take it he doesn't know that Jack is his son."

Liza choked. When she caught her breath again, she asked, "How...how did you know?"

"You said yourself I'm smart. It doesn't take a Phi Beta Kappa to figure out that you two share some sort of history, something a bit deeper than friendship with the Gallaghers. Although I have to admit, I was hoping I was wrong. Besides, I've met your son. Except for your coloring, he's the spitting image of Gaston."

An icy chill ran through Liza's veins at the thought of Jacques discovering the truth. She remembered how cold his eyes had grown, how unfeeling his voice had been when she had posed the hypothetical question of an unplanned pregnancy years before. Even now she could still remember the hardness in his expression when he insisted he would have the pregnancy terminated before bringing any child fathered by him into the world.

"What surprises me is that he didn't figure it out himself the minute he saw Jack."

"He's never met Jack. In fact, he doesn't even know I have a son."

Robert let out a low whistle. "You've got to be kidding? You can't keep something like that a secret, Liza. I'm surprised you've managed it this long. Anyone who knows you knows about your son. I can't believe someone hasn't already said something about him in front of Gaston."

"I've been very careful and made sure I spent as little time in Jacques's company as possible."

Robert frowned. "I don't know, Liza. Seems to me it's a dangerous game you're playing. What are you going to do if he finds out?"

"He won't find out," she said with more conviction than she was feeling. "Besides, in another week the gala will be over and he'll be gone. Until then, I'll just go on being careful." And hope she could continue to manage resisting Jacques. Panic began to bubble inside her again at the thought of Jacques discovering the truth. She couldn't risk Jacques's rejection of their child. "Please, Robert. Promise me you won't say anything to him."

"I think you're making a mistake, Liza. If I were Gaston, I'd want to know that I had a son. I'd be plenty angry that you hadn't told me a long time ago." He paused. "It might make a difference."

"What might make a difference?" Jacques asked, moving to stand beside Liza.

Liza tensed. Her stomach churned mercilessly, fearful of how much he had heard. She tried to think of something to say, but her tongue was like lead in her mouth, unable to move.

Prying the wineglass from her fingers, Jacques gave her a quizzical look as he handed her a fresh glass. "Ginger ale," he informed her, obviously thinking she meant to refuse.

"Thank you," she finally managed to say despite the thickness in her throat.

"What is this thing that you think will make some difference?"

Robert's gaze shifted from Jacques to her and back again. "I was suggesting that we announce tonight that I've made a preliminary bid on that sculpture you donated for the silent auction. In all likelihood, most of the people here will be the ones bidding on it the night of the gala. A little early competition might be good. It might drive up the interest and the price."

Liza sent a grateful look in Robert's direction, and when he gave her an encouraging smile she made an effort to relax. Thank heavens, she thought, Jacques hadn't heard them. What would she have done if he had? What would she do if he did find out he had a son? Would he hate her? Would he look at Jack and see the darkness in their son that he believed he saw in himself? Liza fought back a shudder at the thought.

"It makes sense to me. What do you think, Liza?" Jacques asked.

She jerked her attention back to him. "I...I guess it would be okay."

"Good, then it's settled," Robert said, making her almost believe that they had actually been discussing something as simple as the silent auction.

"Then let's go make the announcement and get the ball rolling," Robert suggested, favoring her with another approving look before moving to her side. "You'll excuse us, won't you Gaston?" Without waiting for an answer, he guided Liza to the front of the room and called for everyone's attention.

Thirty minutes later, Liza slipped out of the living room of the Carstairs mansion and into the study. Closing the door behind her, she leaned against it, grateful to shut out the hum of voices, the tinkling of glasses and china, her awareness of Jacques. Making her way silently across the cream-colored carpet of the impeccably decorated room, Liza breathed a sigh of relief.

Dear Robert, she mused. He had been right. The impromptu announcement that he intended to add Jacques's piece to his extensive art collection had served to heighten the interest of the other collectors present. And no doubt the bidding at the auction for the work on the night of the gala would be fierce. Liza smiled as she considered what that would mean to the summer camp for the kids.

And of course Jacques's presence, his encouragement that the people be generous and think of the children hadn't hurt, either. In truth, it was Jacques's own generosity that had made it all possible. Gratitude and pride rushed through her as she thought of the children who would benefit from his selflessness. Though he had claimed to have done it for her, Liza knew better. She had heard too many stories from Peter and Aimee over the years of Jacques's generosity. Besides, hadn't she herself witnessed firsthand his impassioned plea to the media for support of the fund-raiser?

Why then, Liza asked herself as she had so often in the past, would a man who was so giving and who brought so much light to people's lives, consider himself incapable of loving anyone because of a darkness inside him?

The answer was the same one she had reached three years ago. Because it wasn't a matter of Jacques not being able to love, but simply a case of his not loving her. The realization, though not new, sent a fresh shaft of pain through her just the same.

Moving to the window, Liza gazed out into the beauty of the winter night. Stars dusted the sky, twinkling against the canvas of black. The moon glowed like a huge glass ball suspended in space, glistening on the freshly fallen snow. In just over a week it would be Christmas.

And by then Jacques would be gone. The speed and sharpness of the ache that came with the thought surprised her, making her feel lonelier than she had in a long time. Liza hugged her arms around herself. Had she been fooling herself these past few weeks? Deep down inside had she secretly been hoping that he would stay?

"A lovely picture, isn't it?"

Liza spun around and spied Jacques standing a few feet away. She had been so tangled in her thoughts she hadn't even heard him enter the room. "Yes," she finally managed to say, making an effort to keep her voice cool despite the frantic beating of her pulse. She turned back to stare out the window. "There's something beautiful about seeing everything covered with snow at this time of year."

"That is because it looks like one of your Christmas cards."

Cocking her head to the side, she considered that. "Yes, I guess it does."

"And I remember how much you like Christmas."

The words were a soft whisper against her neck. Liza could hear the smile in his voice, see it in his eyes as she caught his reflection in the window's glass when he moved to stand behind her. "Everyone likes Christmas," she said, steeling herself against the warmth of his nearness and her feelings for him.

"Not the way you do. I remember the way you smiled when we plugged in the Christmas tree that year, the way your eyes glowed when you saw the wrapped package under the tree. More than anything, I wished that I could have afforded to buy you a dozen gifts that Christmas just for the simple pleasure of watching your face light up when you opened each package."

Liza swallowed. Her heart pounded wildly. A buzzing started in her head at the yearning she saw in his eyes and the regret. She tore her gaze away from his image, determined not to be caught in the maelstrom of memories. "I didn't want a dozen gifts, Jacques." All she had wanted was him.

"But I wanted to give them to you just the same. I wish you would let me give them to you now."

He turned her around to face him, touched her face with his fingers. The simple movement sent a surge of heat and longing through her.

"Why did you send back the scarves, Liza?"

"Because I couldn't accept them."

"You accepted the flowers, the fortune cookies."

"Because it would have been too much trouble to try to send them back, and you wouldn't have been able to get a refund even if I did. But the scarves were a different story. They were too expensive, Jacques. You shouldn't have sent them. In fact, you shouldn't have sent any of the gifts. I wish you would stop."

"I do not want to stop. I can afford to give you expensive things now, which I could not do three years ago."

"But I can't accept them from you."

"Why not?" he asked, disarming her by sliding a strand of hair behind her ear and stroking her lobe in the process.

Liza fought the shiver of sensation that rushed through her at his touch. She kept her eyes open, when she wanted to shut them. She kept her back stiff, when she wanted to lean against him. "Because a gift like that, it's too...too personal."

He smiled at her, then smoothed his finger from the tip of her ear, along the line of her jaw. "It was meant to be personal."

"But there's nothing personal between us anymore."

"Liar." To prove his point, he moved a fraction closer. His lips curved when she took a step back and came up against the windowsill.

She hiked up her chin, determined not to give in to the dizzying sensation that was building inside her. His fingers never stopped, just continued in a lazy journey down her neck, her ribs, the dip in her waist, the curve of her hips. Then he began retracing the path. "We can't go back, Jacques."

"Who wants to go back?" He brushed his mouth against her ear and whispered, "The present suits me just fine."

Liza clamped her lips shut to cut off the moan that had risen in her throat. His fingers inched their way upward to the sides of her breasts. She braced herself, determined not to let him know just how badly she wanted to feel his hands close around her, how much she wanted to press her aching nipples into his palms. "You're wasting your time, Jacques," she said, surprised she could sound so calm when inside she was splintering. "You're not going to change my mind. I'm not going to go to bed with you."

"No?"

"No," she told him firmly, only to realize too late her own mistake. She had challenged him, and Jacques Gaston was not a man to refuse a challenge—especially not one issued by a woman. He was too experienced, too adept at the workings of the feminine mind and body to do otherwise. His pursuit of her three years ago had been proof enough. His relentless attempts to seduce her during these past few weeks had merely confirmed it. Silently Liza cursed her own stupidity.

Cupping her chin in his hand, he tipped up her face, and Liza caught the mocking gleam in his eyes. "It appears I will have to work harder on changing your mind."

And before she could object, he was fitting his mouth to hers, tasting, teasing, tempting. Slowly he traced his tongue along the line of her mouth, the seam of her tightly closed lips. Liza forced herself to remain rigid against the onslaught, willing her fingers not to slide into his hair, not to press her body closer to him.

"Open for me, sweet Liza."

Her stomach quivered, but she held her ground, reciting the words to Jack's favorite cartoon song in her head to keep from responding. She had to prove to Jacques that she was unaffected by his kiss.

Then he nipped her bottom lip. Liza gasped in surprise

and Jacques took advantage by moving in. He continued to tease her, to tempt her, to try to seduce her with his mouth and his tongue. Desperate, Liza began another series of mental gymnastics to keep herself from responding. She had moved from the names of the seven dwarfs to those of Santa's reindeer.

Blitzen. Blitzen. Who comes after Blitzen? Liza struggled, feeling her control begin to slip with each stroke of his clever tongue. Her head swam and she was just about to give up on the reindeer, when Jacques lifted his head.

Liza drew in a deep breath and as her vision began to clear, she noted Jacques's stunned expression. Something hot and dangerous flickered in his eyes, and he started to touch her again.

Quickly Liza stepped out of his reach. "Like I said before, you really are wasting your time trying to seduce me," she told him coolly, praying her legs wouldn't prove what a phony she was by buckling beneath her before she could make it out the door.

"It's not over, Liza."

"Yes, it is. Sorry if that hurts your ego, but that's the way it is." Gripping the doorknob for support, she told herself to make it good. Make him believe she was no longer interested in him. She angled her chin up another notch and looked back over her shoulder at him. Feigning a coolness she was far from feeling, she quipped, "You might want to give Melanie Stevens a try. She's the striking redhead in the black cat suit. She's had her eye on you all evening."

Damn her. She had been right, Jacques admitted silently. She *had* done a number to his ego. Anger and frustration surged through him as he recalled Liza's response to his kiss. He had been so drunk on the taste and feel of her in his arms that it had taken several long moments before he realized that while his mind and body were going up like a whiff of smoke, she was as cool and unaffected as a piece of stone.

Damn her. Jacques snagged the glass of whiskey he had ordered from the bar. He had spent a lot of time in the company of women, known too many females intimately—including Liza—not to expect more than tolerance of something as personal as a kiss. Hell, a slap to his face would have been preferable to that bored and distracted look she had given him.

Frustrated, he took a swallow of the whiskey and tracked Liza's movements about the room. Dammit, he had a reputation as a man who loved women—a reputation he had rightfully earned. And while not all of those women had tumbled into his bed, a fair share of them had—including Liza. Not even the cool "touch me not" princess she had been three years ago had been *that* unaffected. And she certainly hadn't been so cool and controlled when he had kissed her last week.

"There's someone else."

Her words ran through his head again and Jacques experienced that quick one-two punch to the gut. Once more he shoved the notion aside. He refused to believe it. She was lying. She had to be. Not once in the five weeks since their paths had crossed again had he seen any evidence of another man save Carstairs. He watched as Carstairs, his hand at Liza's back, led her to another trio of guests. Jealousy stirred inside him, digging in its claws.

Scowling, Jacques turned away. He tossed back the last of the whiskey and palmed the glass, debating whether to have another. He thought of his father, of the times he had seen the other man's mood shift from charming to angry to downright mean with each dip in the bottle. Remembering the ugliness that followed, Jacques set down his glass.

"Hello again."

Jacques shook off the memory and turned to face the owner of the deep, sultry voice—Melanie Stevens, the stunning redhead whose name Liza had tossed out to him. "Mademoiselle Stevens." Jacques inclined his head.

She arched one brow. "Robert barely introduced us before he whisked you off to meet someone else. I didn't think you'd remember my name."

"I never forget a beautiful woman's name." Jacques flashed her a smile, more because it was expected than because he actually wanted to.

"You're a dangerous man, Jacques Gaston." She smiled at him, her hazel eyes twinkling with pleasure and anticipation. "Fortunately, I'm a woman who likes danger. If you've had your fill of rubbing elbows with the monied gentry, I know a place that serves a mean Black Russian and some pretty hot jazz. Interested?"

As invitations went, it was a good one, and he had no doubts that if he took the sexy redhead up on her offer, he wouldn't spend another sleepless night tossing and turning alone in his bed.

Only it wasn't the sexy redhead he wanted. Or any of the equally sexy blondes or brunettes who had crossed his path during the past month. He wanted Liza. His gaze strayed to the cool, green-eyed blonde across the room. It's revenge and lust, he told himself, had been telling himself for the past month. But he had a sick feeling in the pit of his stomach that he was lying to himself.

The thought scared the hell out of him.

He shifted his attention back to the woman before him. He should run like hell, take the luscious Melanie up on her offer and let her help him forget about Liza.

He couldn't do it. Jacques raked a hand through his hair with unsteady fingers. Despite what many people thought, what he had encouraged them to believe, he didn't use women. He couldn't use this one. "You are a gorgeous woman, Melanie Stevens, and someday when I am an old man, I am sure I will regret this. But I am afraid I am going to pass."

"You're sure?"

Jacques found himself laughing out loud. He suspected Melanie Stevens had seldom had a man turn her down before. "I am afraid so."

Tipping her head slightly she glanced in the direction where his attention had been focused—to where Liza stood with Robert Carstairs and another couple. "Other plans?"

Jacques thought about that a moment. "If I am lucky, yes."

Her lips spread into a mischievous smile. In her tight-fitting cat suit with her painted mouth and sultry eyes, she reminded him of a naughty kitten. "Hmm. Well, since your interests lie elsewhere, maybe I can do us both a favor and see if Robert's in need of some consolation."

Jacques watched Melanie saunter off and neatly cut Robert away from the group before deciding to make his own move. They had been here for more than two hours, surely they could leave now, he thought as he started in Liza's direction. Although she had insisted she was going to drive home, he had no intention of allowing her to do so—at least not alone.

God, he wanted her. Was it possible to want someone so much and for them not to feel the same? He sincerely hoped not. Because he was about to go insane with the wanting and waiting.

"Jacques, there you are," Jane Burke said, spotting him just before he reached Liza. "There's someone here I'd like you to meet...."

After being snagged by Jane and a group of bankers standing directly behind Liza, Jacques nodded at something that was said without even having heard and then he excused himself. He started to cut in on Liza's conversation with a silver-haired matron named Mrs. Aber-something-or-other, whom he'd met earlier, when the other woman asked, "And how is Jack? Still as handsome as ever I bet?"

"He's too handsome for his own good if you ask me.

But he's fine," Liza replied, her voice growing soft and warm. "We're going to pick out our Christmas tree tomorrow."

Jacques froze. Ice skidded down his spine.

"It's been ages since I've seen him. Why don't the two of you come by for lunch."

"We'd love to. Maybe after the holidays," Liza said. "With the gala so close and Christmas next week, things are a little crazy."

Jealousy and anger whipped through him, striking him equal blows. He shoved his hands into his pockets to keep from grabbing her. "Liza," he said, his voice cold, clipped. "Are you ready to go yet?"

She spun around; her face paled as she looked at him. "I...yes." She turned back to the other woman. "Good night, Mrs. Abernathy. Thank you for coming."

"Anytime, dear. Give Jack a hug for me."

He followed her to the foyer in silence. Careful not to touch her, afraid of what he would do if he did, Jacques helped Liza on with her coat. Opening the car door for her, he slammed it closed hard enough to cause several heads to turn. He didn't care. He couldn't care.

He slapped the stick into gear and sent the car speeding down the driveway, causing the wheels to squeal on the icy road. He drove in silence, too angry to speak to her, to even look at her.

Jack. There really was another man and his name was Jack. Jealousy grabbed him by the throat and wouldn't let go. Jacques wrapped his fingers around the steering wheel, anger building inside him.

He turned the car onto the icy road that led back to the city, taking the curve too fast. Liza screamed as the car slid off the road. Jacques held on to the wheel and worked the brakes, bringing the car to a sudden halt less than a foot from the trunk of a large tree.

"Have you lost your mind?" Liza cried out as she stared

at the tree in front of them. Her eyes were wide and frightened, her face deathly white.

"Maybe I have," he told her angrily. "It would not be the first time I have gone crazy because of you."

"Because of me?" she repeated, shocked. Her hands curled into fists. "You bastard! You're blaming me? You could have killed us both."

Too blinded by his own swirling emotions, he didn't see the fist coming. She caught him on the jaw with a right hook. Fury, pain exploded. Jacques grabbed her wrists, dragged her to him. "Who is he, Liza? Who in the hell is Jack?"

...

Seven

"**T**ell me," Jacques demanded.

Liza's body tensed and she jerked her wrists free of his grasp. Aided by the dim light from the car panels and the sliver of moonlight through the window, Jacques watched her face, saw her struggle to even her breathing, to bring her temper under control. Within moments, she had her cool, tidy expression back in place. The fact that she could do this so easily when his own emotions were scattered and raw only infuriated him more. "Dammit, Liza. Tell me who the hell Jack is."

"You don't know him."

Jealousy and pain ripped through him again as he heard that soft note creep back into her voice. A tortured cry, more animal than human, escaped his lips as the black mist of rage enveloped him. His control snapped. Jacques grabbed her by the shoulders, dug his fingers into the thick wool of her coat. "Look at me, dammit. Tell me who he is and what he is to *you*."

She looked at him out of those cool green eyes. "He's someone I love very much."

Her words were a blow, more effective than any punch. Jacques nearly doubled over at the pain that sliced through him. "You are lying."

"No, I'm not. It's true, Jacques. I love him."

Temper torched, whipped through him like a hungry blaze. He tightened his fingers on her shoulders. He wanted to shake her, make her admit she wasn't telling the truth. He shoved her away from him instead. Furious, hurting, he punched the dashboard of the car. Pain shot up his arm, a powerful, mind-bending pain that caused him a wealth of hurt, but it didn't come close to the hurt inside him. He lifted his fist, ready to go another round with the dashboard. Anything to blot out the ache he was feeling inside.

"Jacques!" Liza grabbed his fist before he could use it again. "Stop it! Look what you've done to yourself. You're bleeding."

"I am bleeding inside, damn you." He had believed her three years ago when she had told him she loved *him.*. That she would always love him. Only he hadn't realized until now just how much that had meant to him, how much he had counted on her always loving him. It wasn't fair. He had nothing to offer her—not love or even himself. But he wanted, no, he needed to know that she still loved him.

"I don't think it's broken. But of all the idiotic things to do." She fumbled in her bag, pulled out a handkerchief and started to wrap his bleeding knuckles. "This isn't even your car. What are you going to tell them at the rental agency when they see that dent—"

"I do not care about the car or the rental company." He snatched the fingers trying to minister to him. "I do not believe you, Liza. I will not believe you. You are lying. You cannot love him. You said you would always love *me.*" Frantic, Jacques grabbed the labels of her coat and pulled her to him. "Tell me you are lying, Liza. Tell me you do not love this Jack."

Her bottom lip quivered. "But I do love him," she whispered.

Jacques squeezed his eyes shut as emotions ripped through him with the force and fury of a blizzard. When he opened them again, all he could see was the brilliant green of her eyes. He would not, could not let her go. Cursing her, cursing himself, he yanked her even closer, bringing her face to within inches of his own. Angry, he said, "Tell me, Liza. Does your Jack turn your blood to fire the way I do?"

When she didn't answer, he gave her a little shake. "Does he?" he demanded.

"No."

Too angry and aching to even enjoy that triumphant tidbit, he continued to push her. "And when he kisses you, does he make you feel the way I do? Does he make you feel like this?"

"Jacques, don't—"

But he cut off her protest with his mouth. He captured her trembling lips, taking them, ravishing them in an angry, punishing kiss, refusing to believe he could feel so much and she so little. He plundered, he took, he demanded a response from her.

When he felt her tremble, heard the moan deep in her throat, satisfaction surged through him. And then he could no longer think, he could only feel as the ice gave way to flame. Then it was Liza who was demanding. Liza was the one who was curling her fists in his hair, grinding her mouth against his.

Tongues stroked, twined, in a frenzied duel that left neither of them the victor. When her teeth came down sharply on his lower lip, Jacques shuddered and repeated the maneuver on her.

He was dimly aware of the hum of the car's engine, of

the flakes of snow splattering against the windshield. But the fire that had started to burn inside him when he had first seen her again five weeks ago had him in its grip. He had to have, he had to feel himself buried inside her sweet warmth. He had to know that she was his, just as she had been his three years ago.

Dizzy with need, he jerked his mouth free and began to work on unfastening her seat belt. There would be no waiting for the comfort of a bed. He couldn't wait that long. He had waited three years too long already. His fingers trembled as he continued to fumble with the seat belt's latch. "I knew you could not love him," he told her, triumphant.

"What?" Liza asked, her voice husky with arousal.

"I knew you did not love this Jack, that you still loved me," he told her as he finally released the seat belt. He started to reach for her.

Liza caught his bruised hand. "No, Jacques. Wait."

"But, Liza—"

"No. Don't. Please."

The alarm in her voice, the sudden stillness of her body had him yanking his gaze up to her face. Desire died. The blood in his veins turned to ice when he saw what he had done. That beautiful delicate mouth of hers was swollen. A drop of blood trickled at one corner, an ugly red stain against the soft white of her skin. "*Chérie*, I am sorry." He started to press his finger to the bruised flesh. "I never meant to—"

She flinched, strained away from his touch. He stared at her face, the evidence of his brutality. He swore, first in French, then in English. He buried his head in his hands as he remembered another woman's tear-stained face, another woman's swollen mouth. And he remembered the black hatred that had consumed him, that had him dragging his father away from the serving maid and shoving him up against a wall.

Along with the memory, his father's angry words came flashing back to him....

"You think you're so much better than me," his father had said.

"I am better than you. That's why I'm leaving." One more day, Jacques told himself. Just one more day. After his mother's funeral, he would leave his father and this cursed house forever.

"Go ahead, turn your back on me, on your heritage. Leave. But it will not change who you are, what you are. You will still be Jacques Gaston. My son. The spawn of my seed. That's right, my boy. It is my seed that's given you that handsome face and strong body that the ladies like so much. And it is my seed that has given you the darkness in your soul."

Releasing his grip on his father's shirt, Jacques watched the other man slide to the floor. "I may look like you, but I am nothing like you. I will never be like you."

Etienne Gaston laughed. He looked up at Jacques from where he lay sprawled on the floor. "You think not?" He wiped the blood from his mouth and smiled. "Take a look at yourself. Barely sixteen years old, but you've already got the Gaston temper. Your mother's mollycoddling may have suppressed the darkness inside you for a while, but even she could not stamp it out. Nothing can. It is still there, my boy. Mark my words. It is as much a part of you as I am."

Jacques wrenched himself from the past. His father had been right. The darkness was a part of him, just as his father had said it would be. Just as he had always known it would be. How many times had he felt it, tasted its bite in the throes of temper? Hadn't he witnessed it just now in his rage with Liza? How could anything but the ugly darkness inside him have caused him to be so brutal, such a savage, with Liza?

He looked up at her again. The shock and disgust in those green eyes tore at him, making him feel like the beast he was. "God, Liza. I am sorry. So sorry." He scrubbed a hand over his face.

Chagrined by her wanton behavior, Liza barely registered Jacques's words. She turned away from him and made an effort to steady her breathing. She'd lost it. Completely. What hope did she have now of convincing him he meant nothing to her? Why would he believe her after she'd behaved like some sex-starved female, going up like dry timber to flame with nothing more than a kiss?

"Your mouth. Your beautiful mouth." He started to touch her, then pulled his hand back. "I swear I never meant to hurt you."

Still shaken by her own actions, Liza flicked her tongue to the corner of her mouth, touched the tender spot with her fingertip. She flushed at the tiny smear of blood. Shame washed through her as she thought of her brazen response, the way she had practically attacked him.

"I am sorry," he told her again.

Angry with herself, with him, she snapped, "Forget it. It's nothing. We both lost our tempers and went a little crazy. I'd like to forget it even happened."

"But I cannot forget. How can I? How can you? I behaved like a savage."

And so had she. Liza wanted to cringe. "You proved your point, didn't you?" she said, her voice clipped, too angry with herself to recognize the extent of his torment. "You wanted to prove to me what an expert lover you are. To have me admit that there has never been anyone else like you. Well, I admit it, Jacques. No one has ever made me feel the way you do. I doubt that anyone else ever will again. Are you satisfied now? Does it make you happy to know what an unforgettable lover you are? Does it?"

"Liza—"

Jacques turned at the sudden flash of light at the car's window, then swore at the tap that followed with a deep voice saying, "State police."

Jacques pressed a button and the window on his side of the car slid down, letting in a blast of cold air and a flurry of snowflakes.

"You folks having car problems?" the state trooper asked, his gaze traveling from Jacques to Liza and back again.

"No, Officer. We just took that last curve a little too fast," Jacques replied.

The trooper's gaze scanned the inside of the car and stopped on Jacques' battered hand.

"I'm afraid we got knocked around a little bit," Liza explained.

"Better put your seat belts on and take it slow. Weatherman's predicting another six inches of snow before morning."

"Thank you. We will," Liza said.

Tipping his head, the officer turned and went back to his own vehicle.

Moments later Jacques eased the car back out onto the road. In the interior of the car, only the swish of windshield wipers broke the dark silence, but the air was ripe with charged emotions and things that had been left unsaid.

Liza huddled into her seat, not sure whether to be grateful or disappointed that there were no more innuendos, no more blatant or subtle attempts on Jacques's part to seduce her.

It was just as well, she decided. Now that she'd had a chance to rein in her own emotions, she realized just how upset Jacques had been with himself over his loss of temper. The torment she sensed in him wrenched at her heart, battering her resistance as nothing else could. She didn't need him to tell her that the savage kiss they had shared had triggered some painful memory for him from the past. The utter shock on his face, the self-revulsion she'd heard in his voice when he'd cursed himself, had told her that for him the incident was somehow tied to the darkness he saw in himself.

Twenty minutes later when Jacques pulled the Mercedes into the slot next to her car in the parking garage, he cut the engine. He turned to her, his amber eyes solemn, his mouth giving no hint of the smile that usually came so easily. "I realize I have given you no reason to trust me, especially after the way I behaved earlier. But I wish you would consider staying at the apartment tonight. I do not like the idea of you driving home in this snow," he continued. "There are many rooms, and I give you my promise that if you stay, you will have nothing to fear from me."

The pain and self-reproach in his voice tore at her. "I'm not afraid of you, Jacques."

"Then you should be. Look what I did to you." He stared at her mouth a moment before looking away. "I am sorry, Liza. I never meant to hurt you."

"You *didn't* hurt me, Jacques. You couldn't hurt me or any woman—not intentionally. How could you? You love women. All women," she added, trying to use humor to lighten his mood. From his dark expression, she surmised it hadn't worked. "It's just not in your nature to do anything to deliberately hurt me or any woman."

"That's what I have always told myself. Tonight my actions proved otherwise. God, you must hate me. I hate myself for the way I behaved." He rubbed the heels of his hands against his eyes.

Liza caught his hands, forced him to look at her again. She skimmed her fingers over his scraped knuckles. "I don't hate you, Jacques. I could never hate you."

Emotion darkened his eyes, turning them a deep gold. "Then tell me what it is you *do* feel for me, Liza." When she didn't respond, his fingers tightened around hers. He searched her face. "Tell me, Liza. Please."

"I love you," she admitted. What would be the point in

lying about it when her body had betrayed her feelings to him already?

He squeezed his eyes shut a moment, and Liza felt the shudder that went through him. When he looked at her again, his eyes shimmered with heat. "I have dreamed of hearing you say those words to me again. Even when I told myself I hated you for leaving me, I still wanted you. There has never been anyone else like you. I have missed you so much, *ma chérie*."

"I've missed you, too."

"I need you, Liza."

The words made her heart sing. How many times had she longed to hear him tell her that he needed her, that he loved her. No, she corrected herself. He hadn't said he loved her. At least not yet. But surely he would.

Drawing her to him, Jacques murmured something in French and kissed her slowly, lovingly. He planted kisses on her eyes, her cheeks, her mouth. Tender kisses, gentle kisses, each one slower, softer than the one before. It was as though he was trying to wipe out any memory of the kiss he'd taken in anger. Liza leaned into him, giving in to the dizzying pleasure of being in his arms.

"Ah, Liza." His breathing grew ragged as he continued to make love to her with his mouth. "We have wasted so much time you and I. Let us not waste any more."

No. She didn't want to waste any more time, either. She had wasted three years too long already. Three years when they could have, should have, been together. She would tell him the truth. That he was a father. That they had a son. "Jacques, I...we need to talk."

Groaning, he set her away from him and drew in a deep breath. "We will talk back at the apartment. As much as I want you, I am not going to make love to you in the front seat of a car." He started the car engine.

"Wh-where are you going?"

"Back to the apartment."

"But I can't. I mean, I have to go home," she told him.

Jacques frowned. "Why? You can stay with me at the apartment tonight. Tomorrow we will go to your place and get some of your things."

"Some of my things?" she repeated, feeling as though she were in a daze.

"Yes. Since I will only be here for another week, I had hoped you would want to spend it with me."

The fragile dreams she'd begun to spin in her head crumbled like dust. "I take it when you said we had wasted too much time, you meant that we had wasted time by not resuming our affair when you first came to Chicago."

"Yes, of course." He sighed. "But we still have this next week. I will be here until Christmas."

Suddenly cold, Liza pulled away from him and wrapped her arms around herself. "And then?"

"And then we can try to make sure that our paths will cross often. I am in Chicago at least once a year." Jacques narrowed his eyes. "What is wrong, Liza? You have said you love me, that you do not love this Jack. And yet—"

"I never said I didn't love Jack."

Jacques's lips tightened into a thin line. An angry muscle ticked in his cheek. "Do you love him?" he spat out the question.

"Yes. I do."

"You expect me to believe you are in love with both of us?"

"It's true."

Jacques turned from her. He gripped the steering wheel and swore. "Then you will have to choose. I will not share you, Liza. Not even for a little while. Either you love me or you love him."

Liza's heart pounded. *Say you love me. Tell me you want us to be together always—not just for a quick fling,* she prayed. But he didn't say any of those things. Finally she said, "If I have to choose, then it's Jack that I choose."

Jacques swore. "Why?" he demanded. "You do not wear his ring. You were even dating Carstairs, so it cannot be because he is offering marriage and I am not."

"No. That's not the reason."

"Then why? Why him and not me?"

Her heart twisted at the anguish in his voice. She swallowed. "Because he gives me the one thing that you either can't or aren't willing to give me, Jacques. He gives me his love."

"I care for you, Liza."

Liza shook her head. "Caring and wanting aren't enough. I want you to love me, Jacques. Enough to trust that we can build a life together." When she saw his shuttered expression, Liza realized she had lost even before he said the words.

"Then go to your Jack, *chérie*, because I have no love inside me to give to you or to anyone."

Jacques groaned and pulled a pillow over his aching head at the sound of the ringing telephone. The person who had come up with the expression "Drowning ones sorrows" obviously had never tried following his own advice. Because after forty-eight hours of becoming intimate friends with a bottle of Jack Daniels, he didn't feel a lick better now than when he had started. If anything, he felt worse.

"Thank God," he muttered, when the phone finally stopped ringing. He tossed the pillow aside, then tried to sit up, only to wince as the movement sent another jolt of pain shooting to his head. And whatever American, because he was sure it had to have been an American, had coined the term "Out of sight, out of mind" didn't have a clue as to what he was talking about, either. Because despite the fact that he hadn't seen Liza for four days, not once had he been able to close his eyes without seeing her face.

And he couldn't stop wondering if she was with her Jack. Dammit. He'd known dozens of women, made love to more than a few. One woman should not be able to haunt him this way. Not him. Not Jacques Gaston. He loved women. Loved everything about them. The way their minds worked, the way their bodies differed from his. The way they looked, smelled, felt. And he loved making love to them. Only now, somehow, everything had gotten all screwed up. The only woman he wanted was Liza. And the thought of making love to anyone but her held absolutely no appeal. Zilch. Zip. Zero.

Not even the unexpected dinner invitation from Melanie Stevens had helped. He'd known he was in deep trouble when he'd heard himself turning down her generous offer after the meal. That's when he decided to drown himself with the help of his pal Jack Daniels.

But it hadn't helped, either. Nothing had helped, dammit. Not his work, not another women, not even a sea of liquor. He still had that sick, tight feeling in his chest. It simply wouldn't go away. How in the hell was he supposed to get through the gala this weekend without breaking Liza's boyfriend in two and begging her to stay with him by offering her more than he should?

The phone started to ring again and Jacques snatched it up. The sudden motion sent another jackhammer blow to his head. "Yes," he said through gritted teeth.

"Mr. Gaston, this is Mary Ellen from Ms. O'Malley's office," the bubbly voice said. God, how he hated those cheery people like her right now. "I just wanted to remind you about the interview scheduled at Gallagher Foundation this afternoon for three-thirty."

Jacques looked toward the windows and squinted at the bright sunshine dancing along the glass panes. No. He couldn't see Liza again. Not yet, not until he got himself and his emotions under control. "Thank you for reminding me, Mary Ellen, but tell Ms. O'Malley I will not be able to come. I am sure she will do just fine without me."

"But, Mr. Gaston. You *have* to be there."

"Why?" he asked, frowning at the alarm in the other woman's voice.

"Because this is the interview for the community news publication. They're supposed to interview you and Ms. O'Malley together. They're planning on taking photos of the two of you working with the children."

Jacques sighed as he recalled being told about the photo shoot and accompanying piece several weeks ago. At the time, he had thought it great exposure for Aimee and Peter's charitable foundation, as well as for the fund-raising gala. When the suggestion came up that he participate by giving an art lesson to the children, he had agreed. But his motives had been more selfish than altruistic. He had known it would give him another opportunity to be with Liza.

"Mr. Gaston? Are you still there?"

"Yes, Mary Ellen. I am here."

"What should I tell Ms. O'Malley?" she asked.

"Tell her I will see her at three-thirty."

Hanging up the phone, Jacques gingerly made his way to the shower. If there were any justice in the world, he told himself, Liza was feeling just as miserable as he was.

She didn't look the least bit miserable, Jacques decided, as he watched Liza from the table where he had been working with one of the children in the group of five-year-olds. Feeling restless, he had decided to come early for the interview and help out with the younger group of would-be Picassos. Except for a quick hello that was followed by a tight smile, she had barely looked his way.

He, on the other hand, had difficulty keeping his eyes off her. Dressed in that red suede and leather suit and matching suede boots, she had him thinking of Christmas wishes and fantasies that didn't have a prayer of coming true.

She laughed at something a dark-haired boy said, then

stooped down beside him. The suede fabric tightened across her bottom. Jacques took a deep breath and closed his eyes to shut off the erotic thoughts he was having of stripping off that suit and discovering red lace beneath it.

"Mr. Jacques, are you okay?" the blond pixie he had been working with asked.

"I am fine, *ma petite*. Why do you ask?"

"Because you had a funny look on your face."

He tweaked the girl's nose. "That is because I have a funny face."

The child laughed and went back to work on her picture. And Jacques went back to watching and wanting Liza.

"Ms. Liza, look what I drawed," the tow-haired girl at the next table called out. "It's a Christmas tree."

"And what a lovely tree it is," Liza declared.

"Look at mine," the little girl under Jacques's direction piped in.

Liza turned, and her gaze collided with his for long seconds, before she looked away and came to stand next to the child. "What have you got there, Tori?"

"I've got a Christmas tree, too. And a family. See, there's the mommy, the daddy and the little girl. My mommy says Christmas is a time for families."

Liza's smile withered on her lips. A pained expression crossed her face. Jacques frowned, wondering what had made her so sad.

"Do you like it?" the child asked.

"It's beautiful," Liza said in a voice that sounded husky and thick. A strained smile spread across her lips. "I'm sure your mommy and daddy will love it, too."

He wanted to reach for her, pull her into his arms. He settled for touching her arm. "Liza, are you all right?"

"I'm fine. Thanks," she said coolly, stepping away from his touch.

Her rebuff smarted; still he pushed. "I think we should talk."

"I don't think so, Jacques. I believe we covered everything the other night. Now if you'll excuse me, I just saw
the reporter come in, and I'd like to get this interview over
with. I still have a lot of things to take care of before the
gala this weekend."

Un, deux, trois...

Jacques gritted his teeth and began counting to ten. Im-
pulsive, volatile, quick-tempered by nature, for the next
fifty minutes he exercised a patience that he was proud of.
He answered questions, posed with children for photo-
graphs, gave a quick lesson on watercolors. He listened as
Liza detailed the merits of the Gallagher Foundation and
the purpose and goals behind the fund-raising gala that
weekend. He added his own spin on the importance of the
fund-raiser and his support of its efforts.

By the time the infernal session had come to an end,
Jacques had decided to take his best shot. Evidently what
Liza was looking for was a commitment. Whatever she felt
for this Jack fellow, it obviously wasn't strong or she
wouldn't still love him. Given a choice, Liza might be willing to settle for what he could offer her. He couldn't offer
her love—even if he were capable of such an emotion, and
he was quite sure he wasn't, he'd vowed long ago never to
risk the repercussions. Not even for Liza.

No. He couldn't offer her love, but he could offer her
his desire and his fidelity. For a man who'd always taken
great care in selecting partners who wanted the same "no
strings attached" relationship as he did, it was a big step.
It was a commitment. He hoped for Liza it would be
enough.

The photographer began to repack his equipment and
Jacques moved next to her. "Do you think we might go
somewhere for a cup of coffee?"

She hesitated, and Jacques suddenly found himself nervous. He shoved his hands into his pockets. What an odd
position for him to be in, Jacques mused. He'd never had

any problem when it came to speaking to women. But then, there had never been anyone else like Liza. Shaking off the bout of nerves, he pressed, "Please, Liza. I would really like to talk to you."

"All right. Let me get my things first."

"Ms. O'Malley," the teacher who supervised the children's class came over to her. "There's a gentleman here to see you. The good-looking fellow over there by the door."

Jacques looked at the man and then at Liza. Her face lit up. Her eyes glowed. A wide smile spread across her lips. He felt a flash of jealousy and anger, but worse, he felt pain. She hadn't been lying, he realized. She really did love this other man. Something inside him died.

"Jacques, I... Do you mind? That's—"

"No need to explain. Go ahead. It is not important."

She paused. "But I thought—"

"Liza," the man called over to her and waved.

"Go ahead," he told her. "Do not keep your friend waiting."

Jacques stayed, however. Long enough to watch her rush over to the other man, to see her go into his arms, to have him lift her and spin her around. Then he had seen the little boy rush over and the three of them hugging and laughing with one another.

Then he couldn't watch any longer, couldn't bear to see the love shining in their eyes for one another. The picture perfect family they made.

Racing for the side exit, he barely made it into the men's room before doubling over and throwing up. He could blame it on the booze, Jacques told himself, as he rinsed his mouth out at the basin.

But it wasn't the liquor, he admitted to his pasty reflection in the mirror. He splashed cold water on his face. It was Liza and the realization that even if he hadn't completely lost her, he had to let her go.

It had been one thing to pursue her, to try to seduce her into having an affair with him when he had thought she hadn't wanted more. Even after seeing her with those children today he had still convinced himself an affair with him would be enough. But after watching her with the other man and his son, he knew he could never ask her to settle for what little he could give.

He pressed his fist to his chest, feeling as though someone had just ripped out his heart. Someone had. Liza O'Malley. And he'd helped her to do it.

Staggered by the realization, he gripped the edge of the sink. He'd thought he'd been so smart, so clever, engaging in the game of love but never engaging his heart. Even with Liza he had told himself there was no risk. He had taken such care, such pains, to let her know he couldn't offer anything more than passion. To make sure he felt nothing more than passion.

But passion had never felt like this. Passion, even when it ended, had never hurt like this. Nothing in his life had ever hurt like this.

He wouldn't give a name to this feeling he had for Liza. Was afraid to study it too closely. But one thing he did know, he cared for her too much, and feared for himself just as much, to stay.

He had no choice. For both their sakes he would have to walk away.

Eight

"Edward." Liza hugged the handsome, blond Adonis. "What are you doing here?"

"Now is that any way for a little sister to greet her big brother?"

Liza swatted her brother's arm. "In case you haven't noticed, you idiot, I'm not so little anymore."

"Mommy says calling people names isn't nice."

"And your mother's right," she told her nephew, trying to look properly chastened. "And speaking of your mommy, where is she?"

"Elise is in the ladies' room changing Mandy's diaper. We caught the end of your speech. It was good, Sis. Real good. I'm proud of you."

"Thanks," Liza said, flushing under his praise.

"Didn't mean to scare off your friend."

"My friend?"

He inclined his head behind her. "The big guy you were talking to. Looked real intense. Don't tell me *that* was Robert Carstairs. He doesn't quite fit my image of the fine-mannered aristocrat that Mom described.''

Remembering Jacques, Liza whipped around. But he was no longer there. ''No. No, that wasn't Robert. In fact, he and I aren't seeing each other anymore. So tell me,'' she said, changing the subject before he could question her further. ''What are you guys doing here?''

Edward hesitated. His brow furrowed a moment. ''Hoping to have an early Christmas with you and Jack. Mom said you decided not to come home for the holidays this year.''

''It's a really busy time for me. With the gala this weekend and all. Besides, this is our first Christmas in our new home. Last year we were still in an apartment. I want Jack to wake up in his own bed Christmas morning and be able to run out and see what Santa Claus brought him. I want to make some special memories for him to look back on, like the ones you and I had as kids.'' And deep down, she admitted, a part of her had hoped that maybe Jacques could have been a part of those memories. Shaking off the sad thoughts, she gave her brother a smile. ''Anyway, we'll be coming out after Christmas.''

Her brother squeezed her hand. ''I know. But Elise and I will be gone before you get there. That's why we're here. We decided to leave a few days early and stop here first. We thought we'd visit with you and Jack and let you visit with your niece and nephew before we head on to Mom and Dad's for Christmas. Do you mind?''

''Mind? I'm thrilled.'' And she was. She loved her family and was close to them. Even though they hadn't understood or agreed with her decision not to tell Jacques she was pregnant three years earlier, they had stood by her.

''Then having us around for a day or two won't, you know, cramp your style?''

''Cramp my style?'' Liza repeated.

Her brother shrugged and busied himself retying his

son's shoe. "Yeah. You know, get in the way of your social life."

Liza wrinkled her brow. She had a sneaking suspicion there was more behind her brother's visit than he was saying. She was just about to call him on it, when Eddie, Jr., made a dash for the door.

"Mommy! Here we are!"

Liza shifted her gaze to her sister-in-law, who was approaching and holding a tiny dark-haired version of herself with one hand and little Eddie's hand in the other. "Liza, you look fabulous," she said, turning over the children to her husband. "Not that I can remember you looking any other way."

Liza gave the other woman a warm hug. "It's so good to see you."

"I'm glad to see you, too." Elise's brown eyes sparkled as she stepped back from Liza's embrace. "So now, tell me. Is it true what Mother O'Malley says? Have you really taken back up with that scoundrel Jacques Gaston again?"

Edward groaned and scrubbed a hand over his face.

"What's a scoundrel, Aunt Liza?" four-year-old Eddie asked.

"He's a sneaky older brother who, if he values his life, had better mind his own business."

But her brother hadn't minded his business. Back at her home that evening and the next one, after dinner was finished and all the children had been put to bed, Edward ranted and raved, cajoled and pleaded with her. When even his threats didn't work, he threw up his hands.

"I don't understand you, Liza. How could you take up with the man again and not tell him he's the father of your son!"

"I told you it's business between me and Jacques," Liza argued.

"Bull sh—"

"Edward. We agreed no foul language," her sister-in-law reminded him. "Have you forgotten being called to school last week after Eddie, Jr., started repeating in his Pre-K class that last little gem you're so fond of using?"

Her brother clamped his mouth closed; a dull flush colored his cheeks. He turned back to his sister. "You made a mistake not telling the man three years ago when you got pregnant. You're making another one now by not telling him he has a son."

"Maybe so. But it's my mistake to make, Edward. Not yours."

Her brother fumed and paced the length of her living room like a caged tiger. Five years her senior, Edward had been every bit as much a ladies' man as Jacques, before he'd fallen hard for her sister-in-law. Now that he'd married, he'd put all of that energy and passion he'd once expended in playing the male-versus-female game into being a good husband. The man who once claimed he'd remain a bachelor forever now extolled the virtues of matrimony. And evidently, matrimony is what he wanted for his sister.

"Believe me, if Elise had had my child, I'd certainly want to know about it."

"I did have your child, darling. Both of them," Elise reminded him.

"Yeah. But not until *after* we were married." Arms folded across his chest, Edward stopped in front of the chair where Liza was sitting and glared down at her. "A man has a right to know he's a father, to know he has a son."

"Helping to make a baby doesn't necessarily make a man a father," she retorted. And it certainly didn't make a man love the child he'd help to create.

"No. But he at least deserves a chance to decide if he wants to be one."

Her brother was right. Jacques did deserve a chance to decide if he wanted to be a father, Liza admitted silently. Only she was desperately afraid to give him that chance and risk his rejection of their son.

* * *

The next afternoon, when she closed the door after her brother and his family's departure, Liza leaned against it. Her brother's words continued to play in her head.

Jacques did deserve to know, she told herself again. And she'd almost told him, too, that night after the patron party. She blinked back tears as she thought of that dreadful night again and how foolish she had been in thinking Jacques might actually love her. Armed with his love, she would have faced all his ghosts with him, helped him to fight them. But he didn't love her. She'd had to face the fact that night.

Feeling that sharp painful jab near her heart again, Liza pushed away from the door and went to her son's room. She picked up the teddy bear from the floor and placed it next to her sleeping child. Her heart swelled with pride and love as she smoothed back the blond curls from his forehead to gently kiss him. She'd made the right choice, Liza told herself as she readjusted his covers. While she might risk her own heart, she could never risk her son's.

In the distance she heard the telephone ring. Swiping her eyes, she tiptoed out of the room and raced into the kitchen. "Hello," Liza said, grabbing the phone on its fifth ring.

"Liza, it's Aimee."

"Aimee! How are you?"

"I'm fine. Fat, but fine. I look like I swallowed a basketball."

Liza laughed, unable not to respond to the happiness in her friend's voice. "Pregnant women are supposed to look that way."

Her friend gave an inelegant snort. "That's what that old witch-doctor-specialist Peter insisted I go to says, too."

"And how is the beast?" she asked, using the name she'd tagged Aimee's husband with years ago.

"Beastly because the witch doctor agreed with me and says I can travel. I'm only in my fifth month, so I'm not too far along for us to make the trip. Besides, I want Sarah to have a white Christmas.''

Liza could just imagine Peter Gallagher fussing and fretting over her friend. And going right along with her plans. For a man who was so large and powerful in business, he was putty in his wife's hands. "So where are you guys going?''

"To Chicago."

"Chicago?" Liza repeated in surprise.

"Yes. My doctor says it's okay. In fact, we're coming early. So Peter and I will be joining you for the gala.''

"Aimee, *mon amie*. It is good to hear from you. How are you?''

"Forget the small talk, Gaston. What have you done to my best friend?''

Jacques wiped his hands on a towel and surveyed the finished bust of Aimee's daughter. After witnessing Liza with the other man and his child, he'd come back to the apartment and literally buried himself in his work. Not that it had done much good, he admitted. The ache inside him was as deep and dark as a bottomless sea and just as impossible to escape. "I take it you are referring to Liza."

"Of course, I'm talking about Liza. Jacques, what's going on? Once I got past that smoke screen of cheerful prattle she was giving me about the gala and how well ticket sales are going, I could tell she's miserable.''

He moved to the window and looked out, as snow continued to fall on the city. The barren branches of a tree shuddered under a sudden gust of wind, and Jacques was struck by the thought of how much the tree reminded him of himself. Of the way he felt. Cold. Alone. Empty.

"She sounded lower than the belly of a snake.''

Turning away from the window, he moved to stand in front of the blaze in the fireplace. "A snake?" he repeated the word, trying to translate it from English to French in his head.

"Yes. A snake. You know, one of those slithery things that goes sssss and slides around on the ground."

"Ah, you mean a serpent."

"Right. A serpent," she agreed. "Jacques, what happened? I had hoped that with you and Liza working together you would, you know, both finally realize how you felt about each other."

That was just it. He did finally realize that what he felt for Liza was more than he should, more than was safe for him to feel. He would have seen the danger long ago, if he had only allowed himself to look past his own desire and need for revenge. And because he did care for her, he could never ask her to share his life. Even if it weren't for the other man, he'd seen her face when she'd been with the man's son. Liza wanted children, and having children was something he would never risk.

"I don't know why you're both so stubborn. You know what your problem is, Gaston?" She didn't wait for him to answer, but continued, "You're afraid to grow up. Well let me tell you, your gigolo act is wearing thin. Someday you're going to wake up and find yourself all alone. It's time you gave some serious thought to settling down."

"And do what, Aimee?" Jacques demanded, feeling his temper spark, then catch. Not because of Aimee's lecture. They'd been friends too long for him not to be used to her lectures. What set him off was the truth in her assessment of him ending up alone. Because alone was how he'd been his entire life. It was how he was right now, and it was how his life stretched out before him— alone, cold, empty. Just like that tree. He strangled the telephone receiver in his fist. "You think I should get married? Have a couple of kids like you and Peter did?"

"Yes. As a matter of fact, I do."

"Then you do not know me as well as you think you

do. And you are going to be disappointed, Aimee. Because I have no intention of ever doing either. Liza knows that. That is the reason she has, as you Americans say, decided to move on."

There was silence on the other end of the phone for one heartbeat, then two. "Jacques, I—"

"Your housekeeper Mrs. Gunnerson tells me you and Peter will be arriving on Saturday evening for the gala. Do you want me to pick you up at the airport?"

"No. That's all right. We'll take a taxi. And you can stay in the master bedroom. I've told Mrs. Gunnerson we'll take one of the guest rooms."

"All right," Jacques told her, but he had no intention of following her instructions. *He* would be the one to move into the guest room.

"Jacques, there's something else you should know."

Picking up the poker, Jacques stabbed at the burning logs and waited for Aimee to continue.

"Liza will be spending the night at the apartment, too."

Liza's gloved fingers gripped the steering wheel of her car. Easing her foot off the accelerator, she began applying the brakes as she took another turn in the road. She leaned forward, strained to peer at the road ahead between the swish of her windshield wipers as they battled the steadily falling snow.

Darn it, she thought, looking at a sky already growing dark as the afternoon faded. The snow showed no signs of letting up anytime soon. At the rate she was going, she'd be lucky to get to Chicago in time to get ready for the gala, let alone have any time to visit with Aimee at the apartment.

Another blast of snow sideswiped her compact and Liza tightened her grip on the steering wheel. The wind screamed outside, rattling her car's windows, reminding her just how cold it was. Liza shivered and kicked up the thermostat on the car's heater.

Look on the bright side, she told herself. At least she didn't have to worry about driving home in this mess tonight. In truth, she had been dreading the long drive back to St. Charles after the gala. And while the fund-raising committee would have paid for a hotel room for her, she didn't feel right using the money that would otherwise go toward the summer camp. But now that Aimee and Peter had decided to come for the affair, she would be able to stay at the apartment without the awkwardness or, she admitted, the temptation, of finding herself alone with Jacques.

And after tonight she would probably never see him again. A lump rose in Liza's throat at the realization. The piercing ache in her chest that had been a part of her since the night of the patron party, seemed to explode inside her. Liza pressed her fist to her heart, feeling the sting of tears behind her eyes. If only…

No. She screamed the word silently and blinked back the tears. She wouldn't do this to herself. She wouldn't play that dangerous game again of "if only." Straightening her shoulders, she pushed thoughts of Jacques aside.

The wind howled angrily and sent snow whipping across the road. Another chill zipped through Liza's body, causing her to shudder. She shot a glance at the heater and frowned. She shouldn't be *this* cold. Pulling off one of her gloves, she held her fingers up to the air vent. Cold air kissed her already-icy fingertips.

"Great," Liza muttered, flipping off the heater's switch. She gave the steering wheel a thump. Just what she needed. A near blizzard snowstorm, no heat in her car and an evening in Jacques's company in which she would have to smile and pretend to be happy when inside she was miserable. What else could possibly go wrong?

A five-car pileup on the Chicago loop was what could

go wrong, Liza decided, as she retrieved her overnight bag
from the trunk of her car an hour and a half later. Walking
over to the elevator, she stepped inside and pushed the button marked Penthouse.

Another shiver raced over her as the elevator shot up.
God, she couldn't ever remember feeling this cold, Liza
thought, leaning her head back against the wall. She
couldn't wait to sink her body into a nice hot bath.

The elevator pinged and Liza shifted the bag on her
shoulder and pulled out the key Aimee had given her the
previous year. The melancholy strains of Mahler's Sym-
phony no. 5 greeted her as she entered the apartment. Her
gaze strayed from the CD player to the picture window,
and she remembered standing there not long ago, with
Jacques's hands cupping her shoulders, his warm mouth
pressing hot kisses to her neck.

Shaking her head to clear the memory, Liza stepped inside the apartment. "Aimee? Peter?" she called out. "Any-
body here?" After hanging up her coat, she went to the
master bedroom and tapped on the door. When no one answered, she stuck her head inside. "Aimee?"

At the sound of water running in the shower, she pulled
the door shut. Good idea, she decided as she headed toward
the other side of the apartment to the guest room she usually occupied when she visited. A hot bath was just what
she needed. After dumping her bag and purse beside the
closet, Liza all but raced to the bathroom.

The moment she stepped onto the sea-foam-colored tile
floor, she smiled. The room was almost as large as the
bedroom, Liza mused, not for the first time. How many
times had she teased Aimee that a family of four could live
in a room this size? It was an exaggeration, true, but the
room was magnificent. A mirrored vanity with gleaming
pewter trim lined the wall opposite the tub. An onyx statue
of lovers embracing rested on a marble base in one corner.
An exquisite ivory nude carving of a woman's body that

Aimee had framed in a glass-and-pewter box rested on one wall. But it was the huge jade marble tub positioned beneath a skylight that dominated the room.

And it was that tub that she couldn't wait to get into. Liza kicked off her shoes and moved across the room. Turning on the taps full blast, she dumped in a generous amount of the gardenia scented bubble bath from the jar beside the tub. Eager to sink her chilled body into the warm water, she pinned her hair up on top of her head and quickly stripped off her clothes. On impulse, she dimmed the light switches and lit the candles scattered around the tub and vanity. The gleaming pewter-and-glass fixtures winked at her in the flickering light.

Moments later when Liza eased her body into the steaming scented water, she sighed. She flipped on the whirlpool jets. Leaning her head back against the rim of the tub, she closed her eyes and allowed the soothing heated water to swirl around her, wondering if she would ever feel warm again.

Exiting the shower, Jacques grabbed the towel from the rack and briskly rubbed it over his body. He then wrapped the towel around his waist and moved to the mirror in front of the bathroom counter. After combing his hair away from his face, he stroked his jaw, noting the dark stubble. He reached for his electric razor and, not seeing it, he rummaged through his shaving kit, then frowned.

"Damn," he muttered. He must have moved it into the guest bathroom earlier in anticipation of Aimee and Peter's arrival. And evidently, he'd forgotten to move it back when Aimee called to say they wouldn't be coming after all.

As he moved through the living room, the CD player clicked to a new disc, filling the air with the melodious sound of Nat King Cole singing "I'll Be Home for Christmas." Jacques paused outside of the door to the bedroom. Strange, he didn't remember closing the door, Jacques thought, his brow wrinkling before he shrugged off the thought. Given his state of mind these past few days, he was lucky he remembered anything at all. Turning the knob, he pushed open the door and marched straight toward the bathroom.

It wasn't until he stepped inside the room that he noted the pile of woman's clothing lying on the floor, and then he heard the distinctive hum of the tub's whirlpool jets. Jacques's gaze darted to the tub.

He froze. His heart stopped, then started again as he looked at Liza. Lying in the tub, wearing only a veil of frothy bubbles, her head was tipped back, her eyes closed. The hint of a smile curved her lips.

Turn around, get out of here before she opens her eyes and sees you.

He heard his brain issue the command, but his body refused to obey it. He remained rooted inside the doorway, unable to move. The sweet fragrance of gardenias reached out to him, wrapping him in its tempting scent. He tried to swallow, but his throat felt as though it was lined with dust. He couldn't think. For a moment he forgot how to breathe.

Then Liza shifted in the tub, sending the shawl of bubbles dipping past her shoulders to skim the tips of her breasts.

Desire ripped through him, sending the blood pumping hot and furiously through his veins. And Jacques found himself being hurled back in time—back to a steamy night in New Orleans three years before. Back to the night of an autumn rainstorm, to a tiny loft heavy with the scent of gardenias, to the woman who had tempted him to defy fate and risk more than he should.

As though sensing his presence, Liza opened her eyes. He heard her breath hitch, saw her eyes widen in shock. Then he watched that shock turn to awareness as her gaze slid down his naked chest to the obvious bulge in his towel before racing back up to his face.

"Wh-what are you doing here?"

"I forgot my razor." But he made no move to retrieve it.

"Then, get it and g-get out. Before...before Aimee and Peter find you here." She shifted in the tub again, setting the bubbles dancing across the tips of her breasts.

A fresh wave of desire shot through him as his eyes darted to the dark rosy buds. His shaft nudged more insistently against the towel. Jacques squeezed his eyes shut. He curled his hands into fists to keep himself from going to her, from kneeling beside the tub, smoothing the bubbles away from her breasts and taking one of those nipples into his mouth. His body shuddered as desire clawed at him like an angry beast. Wanting Liza was like a deadly fever, one he had contracted three years ago, and one for which there was no cure.

"Jacques, please."

Opening his eyes, he stared at the fading bubbles, the petal-soft skin. Her face was flushed from the steaming water, her green eyes dark with sensual awareness.

"Please what, Liza?" he asked, angry that she could still make him feel this way.

"Please go before Aimee and Peter come," she said. Turning her head away, she reached for the bar of soap and began to lather it on a cloth.

Damn if he didn't even find that snooty way she tilted her nose in the air arousing. He would have laughed if it weren't for the ache that seemed to be growing more painful by the minute. If he didn't know better, he would have sworn his matchmaking friend Aimee had somehow engineered the weather to cooperate with her. "You do not have to worry about Aimee and Peter, Liza. They are not here."

She lifted one leg and proceeded to soap it. His body tightened at the movement. "But they will be soon. It would be embarrassing for us both if they were to find you in here."

It was too much. Like a match to dynamite. Her cool "duchess to peasant" tone, while he was breaking out in a sweat of desire simply watching her soap her leg, sent him over the edge. "Then you have nothing to worry about, *chérie*. Because Aimee and Peter are not coming."

Nine

Liza darted her gaze to Jacques. Feigning indifference had cost her dearly. She could feel the threads of control beginning to fray. So she forced herself to keep her eyes on his face and not ogle his body—his beautiful half-naked body. Long and rangy with just the right amount of muscle, chest and legs that had been kissed by some tropical sun and dusted with dark blond hair. Judging by the way that rich bronze color stretched across his stomach and disappeared beneath the towel, not even a sliver of pale skin broke the line of that tan.

Liza swallowed. Five minutes ago she had been chilled to the bone. Now her skin felt like it was on fire. And it had nothing to do with the water, and everything to do with Jacques and the way he was looking at her—like a leopard that had just cornered his prey. She tipped up her chin, refusing to be intimidated. "What do you mean they're not coming?" she asked, struggling for a cool she was nowhere near feeling.

"It seems it is snowing in New Orleans, and apparently since snow is a rarity down south, it is not something the city knows how to deal with. The airport has been shut down, and all flights have been canceled."

As the full implication of Jacques's words sank in—that the two of them were alone, that they would be alone tonight in the apartment—Liza's grip tightened on the bar of soap in her hand. The soap slipped from her fingers, and it went flying across the room. It landed on the floor at Jacques's bare feet.

Then everything seemed to move in slow motion.

Slowly Jacques stooped to pick up the soap. He looked up at her from his crouched position, his golden eyes darkening to amber as they skimmed over the tops of her breasts, her throat, before zeroing in on her mouth.

Liza trembled. She pressed her teeth into her bottom lip, feeling trapped in the heat of his gaze. Then he was rising, moving toward her like the beautiful powerful leopard he reminded her of. She stared at him, watched the muscles ripple across his wide shoulders and chest, down the taut, flat belly, to where it disappeared beneath the precarious knot of his towel. Desire pooled in her stomach, spread between her thighs as she noted the bulge in that towel.

When he stopped in front of the tub, Liza dragged her gaze back up to his face. The cheekbones in that lean face of crevasses and angles suddenly seemed more pronounced. That mouth of his—so quick to smile, to charm, to seduce a woman—was pulled into a stern line. The muscle ticking in his jaw told Liza just how tightly he was fighting for control. She looked into his eyes, and another stab of desire sliced through her at the savage gleam in those golden eyes. There was temper there, and violence. There was also desire.

It should have scared her. It thrilled her instead.

"Do not look at me like that," he commanded, his voice as harsh as his expression.

"Like what?" Liza asked.

"Like you want me. The same way that I want you."

Liza knew she should tell him he was wrong, say something smart about his high opinion of himself, but the words were a tangled jumble on her tongue that refused to form on her lips. All she could do was stare at him, stare at him and remember, stare at him and want.

Afraid he would see just how she was feeling, how badly she did want him, Liza tore her gaze away from his face. She looked down at his palm, now clenching the bar of soap. It was a strong hand, a man's hand, roughened and calloused from working with marble and clay.

And heaven help her, she remembered the feel of those hands on her body. She remembered the skill and heat of his touch. His fingers stroking her breasts, her hips, dipping between her thighs, slipping inside her. Gentle and coaxing one moment, hot and urgent the next.

Trembling under the deluge of memories, Liza reached for the soap. She swallowed a whimper as her fingers accidentally scraped his palm.

Jacques groaned, the sound an animal cry of pain or anger. Liza wasn't sure which. She didn't have time to decide or to snatch her fingers away before he captured her hand. His fingers closed around her wrist like a vise, sending the soap splashing into the water. He knelt down on the step leading to the tub.

The breath rushed in and out of her lungs. Her heart pummeled in her chest. With fear. With anticipation. With desire.

"Look at me, Liza."

She looked up. Desire sliced through her again at the wild fever in his eyes.

"I can't give you what you want," he snarled.

"I'm not asking you for anything."

"Yes, you are, dammit!" His eyes were dark with anger. He swore in French, then seized her other wrist. "I promised myself a few days ago that I would do something honorable for once in my life. That I would leave you alone, let you go and make a life for yourself with someone who can give you what you want.''

He eased the shackle hold on her wrists, only to slide his fingers up her wet arms, to her shoulders, her neck. Liza quivered under his touch.

"But I am not going to keep that promise." He fisted one hand in the hair at her nape and pulled her closer, bringing her face within inches of his. "I guess there is just no changing the fact that I do not come from honorable stock."

Liza heard the anger and derision in his voice, saw it in his eyes and knew it was directed at himself. "Don't say that, Jacques. It's not true."

"But it is the truth. I cannot escape it. Just as I cannot escape wanting you. And I do want you, Liza. God help me, I cannot *stop* wanting you."

The jets of the tub continued to hum. The water swirled around her naked body, spinning the scent of flowers around her like a web. Her heart raced, making her dizzy. She pressed her hands against his shoulders, meaning to push him away, knowing she should tell him to stop.

"Tell me your eyes lie to me, Liza." She felt a breath shudder through him as he struggled for control. "Tell me you do not want me. Tell me, and this time make me believe it."

"I—I don't want you," she lied. "I told you before, I love Jack," she whispered in desperation.

He stiffened as though she had slapped him. Anger flashed in his eyes. His fingers tightened in her hair. He tugged, causing her body to arch slightly, exposing her neck. He took advantage, pressed his mouth to her throat, to her chin, to the line of her jaw. When his teeth closed on her bottom lip, Liza gasped.

Jacques captured her lips, swallowed the sound with his

mouth. He kissed her passionately, thoroughly, with a skill that bespoke his knowledge of women, his knowledge of her. Every nerve in her body seemed to have shifted, centered in her lips and the feel of his mouth on hers.

She wanted him to stop. She was terrified that he would. Her body shuddered from the onslaught to her senses, making her knees weak, her body tremble. She clung to his shoulders. She whimpered when he lifted his head.

"You may love him," he said, his voice triumphant. "But it is me you want. Me, Liza. Not him."

And then he was seizing her lips again, invading her with his mouth, his taste, sliding his tongue between her teeth. Liza's heart raced faster, making her head spin. She couldn't think. She wasn't sure she remembered how to breathe. She curled her fingers, digging her nails into his chest.

Then it was her arms sliding over his powerful shoulders, twining themselves around his neck. It was her fingers spearing through his damp hair, fisting, pulling his mouth back to hers. She kissed him deeply, hotly, with all the longing and love she'd held inside for the past three years.

Grabbing her by the shoulders, he dragged his mouth from hers. "Tell me now that you do not want me," he challenged.

"I—I can't. Jack and me, it's not what you think. We're not lovers. He and I—"

"I do not want to hear about him. I want you to admit that it is *me* that you want. *Me*. Say it!"

"I want you, Jacques. I love you."

There was victory in his eyes as he reached for her, pulled her to her feet. Water spilled over, streamed down the sides of the jade tub as he touched her first with his eyes and then with his hands. "Save your love, *chérie*. I have no use for it. All I want is your passion."

And all he would offer her was desire. The realization cut, slashed her heart into tiny pieces. She loved Jacques, had always loved him, and knew now she could never love anyone else. She closed her eyes as he kissed her neck, her throat, her breasts.

If she could have nothing else but his passion, then she would settle for passion. For this one night, this last night, she would take the passion he offered her and then she would let him go. And when it was over, she would still have the memories of this last night with him. That, and the child he had already given her, would be enough. It had to be.

Liza's breath hitched in her chest as his mouth moved to her navel. She fisted her hands in his hair, pulled his face back to hers. "If passion's all you want from me, then take it, Jacques. Take it now...before I come to my senses."

He growled. Snagging her by the waist, he pulled her to him and lifted her into his arms. Water dripped from her body onto him, onto the tile floor, onto the thick moss-colored carpet as he carried her into the bedroom. He kissed her hard. She kissed him back, biting, driving her tongue between his lips.

Moaning, he stripped away the comforter and tossed it to the floor. He laid her onto the bed. The mint and ivory satin sheets were cool on her damp skin, but her body seemed to be on fire. Those strong hands of his molded her breasts, stroked her hips, caressed her thighs. And that hot mouth—it seemed to be everywhere, lighting new fires of sensation with each kiss, launching new bullets of desire with each nibble and stroke of his tongue.

It was too much. It wasn't enough. He was going too fast. He wasn't going fast enough. He parted her thighs, inserted a finger inside her, and Liza cried out.

He swallowed her moans with his mouth. When he lifted his head, she arched her body beneath him, feeling as though she would die if she couldn't feel him inside her. "Hurry, Jacques. Hurry," she demanded.

"Not yet. You're not ready."

"Yes, I am," she countered. Wild with need, she snatched the towel covering his hips and reached out to touch him.

"No," he spit out the word as he captured her hand. Breath rushed in and out of his lungs as though he'd just run a long race. He squeezed his eyes shut. "Do not touch me yet. Give me a minute. I want you too badly. If you touch me now, I won't be able to wait."

A surge of feminine power rushed through her, that he could want her so much. Desire kicked up another notch, making her dizzy with anticipation. "I don't want you to wait," she told him, tugging her fingers free. She stroked the velvety tip of his manhood and was thrilled to see him quiver. Then she closed her fist around him, alternately squeezing and stroking his thick hard flesh.

Jacques yelled out something in French, a curse or a prayer, she wasn't sure which. Then he was tumbling her onto her back, spreading her legs apart. He drove into her in one powerful thrust.

Liza caught her breath as he filled her, stretched her. She saw the shock and regret in his eyes. When he started to withdraw, she wrapped her legs around him, taking him deeper, deeper inside her, filling the emptiness. She clenched her muscles around him.

"Sorcière!"

Witch.

His eyes darkened to the burning gold of flames. He grabbed her hips and slammed into her. Again and again. She met each thrust, demanded more.

He feasted on her with his hands, his mouth, his teeth. He took. So did she. She could hear the slap of flesh against flesh, the rasp of quickened breaths. She could smell the scent of gardenias, of soap, of sex.

She wanted, no she needed, to capture it all, she told herself. Record each sensation, each touch, each sound so she could savor them over and over again when he was gone.

Then Jacques lifted her hips, and began to move inside her again. Faster and faster until she could no longer think. She could no longer reason. All she could do was feel. He pushed her higher and higher still, driving her closer to that ball of heat. Suddenly her body exploded in a burst of fire that sent her flying headfirst into the bright flames. Then Jacques was calling her name, clutching her to him as he followed her into the blaze.

Slowly sanity returned to him. And with it came guilt. He'd pushed her too hard, too fast. She'd been so tight, so hot and tight. And he'd spent damn little time drawing out the pleasure for her, making sure she was ready for him. But he hadn't been able to stop himself. When she'd wrapped her legs around him, clutched him inside her warmth…

Damn, he was getting hard again just thinking about it. Sucking in a deep breath, Jacques pushed himself up on his elbows to look at her. Her eyes were closed, and she had a silly grin on her face. But her lips were swollen and there were whisker burns along her chin and neck. He stroked her cheek. "I'm sorry, *chérie.*"

"Hmm?"

"For hurting you,' he said, noticing now that those whisker burns extended to her breasts.

"Hurt me?"

He frowned at the distracted note in her voice. "Look at me, Liza."

Her lashes fluttered and she opened her eyes. They were a sorceress's eyes, dark and dreamy, the deep rich green of shamrocks. He wondered how he could ever have thought they were cool. "I'm sorry if I was too rough."

"Seems to me, *I* was the one who got rough." She

grinned at him and drew her fingertip to a tender spot on his shoulder where she had sunk her teeth into him.

He ignored her attempt to lighten his guilt. He had never been like that with any woman before—so out of control of his own passion—not even with her. "I did not mean to rush things. I wanted it to be special for you. I wanted to drive you crazy with pleasure. Instead you were the one who drove me insane."

"I did?"

"You demolished me, Liza."

"I'm glad." She smiled at him. "Before, when we were together, I always felt so...so helpless. You'd take me to peak after peak even when I told myself I wouldn't let you. But I could never do the same to you. You could hold yourself back until *you* decided to let go. It didn't do much for my ego."

When he started to protest, she pressed her fingers to his lips. "Tonight I liked knowing that I could make you lose control for a change."

"Believe me, you did." He had been so wild for her he hadn't even remembered to use protection. The realization sent a shiver of panic through him. That was something he was *always* careful about. But before he could ask her, she started moving beneath him.

Jacques groaned, forgetting the question as his body reacted to being inside Liza. He nipped her fingers and stared into her eyes. "If you do not stop wiggling that delectable bottom of yours, you are going to see me lose control again," he warned.

"Really?" she replied huskily, then tightened her feminine muscles around him again.

"Really." His laugh turned into a groan and he rolled over onto his back, leaving her atop him.

"We shouldn't do this. We'll probably be late for the gala," she said, even as she moved astride him and began to rock. She looked like a pagan goddess, he thought, with her head thrown back, golden hair tumbling about her shoulders, her eyes closed to half slits and those long pale legs straddling him.

"No probably about it. We are definitely going to be late," he informed her. Reaching for her breasts, he lifted his hips to move deeper inside her.

"How late?" she asked as she rocked her body forward and backward and then repeated the movements.

Jacques groaned. "Very late," he said, his breath coming hard and fast now. Cupping her bottom, he anchored her to him and lost control again.

They *had* been very late, Jacques conceded, once they were at the gala. The problem was he couldn't wait to leave and have Liza all to himself again. That realization annoyed him, almost as much as it scared him.

So he'd deliberately made himself sit through the meal and make flirtatious conversation with the women at his table just to prove to himself that he could. He liked women, had yet to meet a woman he didn't like, he reminded himself. He didn't need to be with any one woman in order to have a good time. He could certainly spend a few hours at this party without Liza and enjoy himself.

But he'd be damned if he was enjoying himself. He watched Liza at the table across from him. She looked so beautiful she stole his breath away. She'd pinned her hair up with some kind of clip to where only little pieces trailed down her neck. The midnight blue dress she wore covered her from the neck down like a nun's habit. Of course, no nun's habit was made of fabric that gently hugged firm breasts, a narrow waist and nicely rounded hips. And certainly no nun's habit had a cutaway back that dipped dangerously close to that waist. Jacques tugged at the collar of his tux shirt, breaking out in a sweat just thinking about all that baby-smooth skin exposed by the back of that dress.

She tilted her head and laughed at something Dan Something-or-other said to her at the next table. Unable to bear another minute of being able to look at her and not touch her, Jacques excused himself and went to reclaim Liza.

Moments later he stood behind her. Touching the back of her chair, he asked, "Would you like to dance?"

She looked up at him over her shoulder. A smile curved her lips. "Excuse me," she told the gentlemen seated on either side of her. Taking her hand, Jacques led her out to the dance floor. Fortunately for him the band had accommodated his urge to hold her by providing a slow, dreamy tune.

"Really, Jacques," she told him as he drew her into his arms. There was laughter in her eyes and in her voice. "That's the fifth time you've asked me to dance. What are people going to think?"

"That I like having you in my arms." He spun her slowly in a circle and pulled her body a little closer. Taking advantage of the fact that they were dancing, he slid his fingers down the bare skin exposed by the open back of her gown.

He felt the tiny shudder go through her, heard that hitch in her breathing. It reminded him of that noise she made when he buried himself deep inside her. The mere thought had him growing rock hard again.

"Watch your hands, Gaston," she scolded when his fingers dipped a little too low.

"I would much rather watch you." He eased himself away from her so he could look into her face. "In fact, how much longer do you think we have to stay? I want to see those witch's eyes of yours turn all dark and smoky again when I am inside you."

Her eyes heated, and she buried her face against his shoulder. "We can't go yet. The silent auction doesn't shut down for at least another hour. And there's still the money to be collected on the items, and the announcements to be done."

"Why don't I see if I can encourage these good people to be generous and hurry things along."

Everyone had been generous, nearly doubling what Liza had hoped the gala would bring in for the children's summer camp. But it seemed no one had been in a hurry to leave—except for her and Jacques.

The steamy glances and stolen kisses, the accidental brushes of his thigh or arm against hers, had done little to improve her patience. By the time the elevator door to the penthouse apartment pinged, Liza was near mad with anticipation. "Jacques, we're here," she managed after tearing her mouth away from his.

The moment the door closed to the apartment, she was back in his arms. And he was doing delicious things to her body, setting off tiny explosions of heat in her, on her, around her, with each touch of his clever hands, each nibble and stroke of his wicked mouth.

Liza fumbled with the buttons of his jacket. She dragged the sleeves down his arm and pushed it to the floor. She reached for his tie.

Jacques caught her impatient fingers and kissed them. "Slow down, *chérie*. We have all night."

"I don't want to waste it," she told him, barely recognizing the voice of this carnal creature as her own. For pity's sake, she told herself, she was the mother of a two-and-a-half-year-old boy and had remained celibate by choice for more than three years.

And tonight is all I'll ever have. It will have to last me a lifetime.

"I assure you, we will not waste it," he whispered into her ear. His breath feathered along her neck, then he moved to her shoulder. "But this time, I will not let you rush me. I want to make this special for you."

"It will be," she assured him as her legs grew weak.

She would have agreed to anything as long as he didn't stop touching her, kissing her.

Scooping her up into his arms, he carried her into the bedroom. A soft glow illuminated the room from the ginger jar lamp beside the bed, giving his eyes that burnished gold tint she found so fascinating.

When Jacques released his hold to slide her to her feet, Liza stood on unsteady legs. Dizzy with desire, she started to go to work on his shirt buttons.

"Patience, *chérie*," he murmured, capturing her fingers yet again. "I want to undress you." Moving behind her, he began kissing her neck. Slowly, oh, so slowly, he wove a path down one shoulder to the center of her back, down to where the dress slashed to her waist.

Liza trembled as he eased down the zipper and nibbled at the sensitive spot from her waist to the edge of her bikini brief. Arrows of heat shot to her center as his mouth retraced his way back up her spine to the other shoulder. Then he began peeling the dress off her shoulders, taking time to kiss each inch of flesh he exposed.

By the time her dress was off, and she stood before him in her panties and hose, her body was quivering with need. She reached for him again, ready to rip off his shirt.

Once again Jacques stayed her movement. "Not yet," he told her as he eased her back onto the bed. After kicking off his shoes, he joined her and proceeded to slowly drive her insane.

Lifting her hands over her head, Jacques began the torture again. He kissed her fingers, her wrists, nibbled his way to her elbow. Lord, Liza thought, she hadn't known her elbows were such an erogenous zone.

"If I release your hands," he said, in a voice that was not at all steady. "I want you to promise not to touch me until I tell you to."

Unbearably aroused, she glared at him, furious at his

ability to remain so in control of himself when her control had deserted her long ago.

He nipped the underside of her arm. "Promise me, *chérie*. Otherwise, we will be here all night."

"I promise," she said coolly, then ruined it by whimpering as his tongue flicked the shell of her ear. He nibbled his way to her neck, her jaw. She turned her head to meet his mouth, only to have him tease her by tracing her lips with his tongue. "Not yet," he whispered, before moving down her throat to her collarbone.

He cupped her breasts, traced the tips with his fingers, then his tongue. When he took the nipple into his mouth, Liza nearly came off the bed. She curled her fingers into the sheets to keep from breaking her promise and reaching for him.

Then he moved lower. Down her rib cage, across her stomach, to the edge of her panties. He moved lower still. First she felt his breath whisper over the thin silk of her panties. Then his tongue began to stroke her through the silk.

Liza cried out. She arched her body as she felt herself climbing toward the peak. Over and over again, she felt the stroke of silk and the heat of his tongue pushing her closer and closer to the crest. Then the first spasms hit. Liza cried out again as her body shuddered with pleasure. She had barely got her breath back when Jacques gently nipped her with his teeth and started the explosions streaking through her again.

"Oh, Jacques, hurry. Please." She tore at the buttons of his shirt, greedily wanting to taste the skin beneath. She scraped her teeth across his nipple.

He swore. Liza jerked her head up as he tossed away his slacks and moved between her legs. He stripped away her panties and entered her. Then he began to move inside her with deep, slow strokes that took her to the brink, tipped her over and then sent her in a free fall of pleasure. Each time she recovered, he began the trek again.

"Please, Jacques," she told him, when she thought she couldn't possibly stand the pleasure any longer. "This time, I want you with me."

And when he drove her to the edge once more, he clutched her to him, called out her name and jumped off the edge with her.

Hours later, exhausted and sated, Liza lay awake wrapped in his arms, cocooned by the warmth of their love-making. She willed the dawn not to come. She didn't want the night to end, Liza admitted, as she burrowed closer to Jacques, pressing her bottom more intimately to him. Because when morning came she would have to say goodbye.

Jacques stirred. His hands began to move in lazy circles over her breasts, along her waist, her hips. She could feel him hardening, pressing against her buttocks. And then those clever fingers of his dipped lower, slipped inside her. First one. Then another.

While his fingers stroked the sensitive bud at her center, she felt his other hand skim her buttocks. Closing her eyes, Liza gave herself up to the dizzying sensations. After all, she told herself, morning was still hours and hours away.

Ten

Morning came much too soon, Jacques decided as he squinted at the bright sun streaming through the bedroom window. But oh, what a night it had been. Noting the empty space beside him, he plopped down again on the bed and stretched. Things had been good between Liza and him three years ago, but it had been nothing compared to last night. He drew in a deep breath and smiled as he caught the whiff of gardenias that lingered on the sheets.

Face it, Gaston. You've got it bad.

And he did, Jacques admitted, as he got out of bed and headed for the bathroom. He'd known a lot of women in his time, some intimately and some not, but none of them came close to making him feel the way Liza did. Turning on the shower, he stepped under the hot spray. The woman exasperated him, even infuriated him at times, but she also made him happier than he'd ever been. And he couldn't imagine his life without her.

Stunned, Jacques froze in the midst of soaping his chest,

then choked as his slackened jaw took in a mouthful of water. Coughing, he staggered to the bench in the shower and slumped down on the seat. He drew several deep, calming breaths. Still shaken by his own thoughts, he leaned his head against the tiled wall and closed his eyes.

He wasn't in love with Liza, he told himself. He couldn't be. He never fell in love with any one woman—at least no more than any other man did when he found himself in the company of a female and the physical chemistry between them clicked. Besides, he reasoned, he'd always been very careful not to bruise any woman's heart and not to let any woman close enough to bruise his.

Only he hadn't been as careful when it came to Liza. Not three years ago. Certainly not now. Water continued to spray, filling the stall with steam, and Jacques struggled to slow the panic beat of his heart.

Imbécile!

He'd been too caught up in his desire for her to recognize just how deep and fast he'd been sinking. Even though he had admitted caring for her, having deep feelings, he'd convinced himself it wasn't love. Cursing himself for his own arrogance, Jacques stepped back under the shower's spray.

It wasn't too late. He wouldn't let it be, he told himself. Reaching for the shampoo, he dumped some on his hair and began to scrub. Liza knew his stance on love and commitment. He didn't offer any. Unlike three years ago, last night she'd made no mention of the future. It wasn't as though she'd asked him for a commitment. She hadn't. Jacques frowned as he rinsed the shampoo from his hair. *She* hadn't offered any this time, either.

Stepping out of the shower, Jacques toweled himself off and moved in front of the mirror to shave. He wiped the steam from the glass.

And if she had offered you her love? If she had asked you for a commitment, what would your answer have been?

Jacques stared at himself in the mirror. But it was his

father's face he saw looking back at him. And he remembered. The cruel laughter. The sting of heavy fists. The sound of his mother weeping.

No. His answer would have been no. It had to be. The darkness stopped with him. He cared for Liza, had feelings for her, strong feelings. But what he felt wasn't love. He wouldn't let it be. No way would he ever allow himself to sink into that trap.

He hadn't sunk yet, Jacques told his reflection. Picking up the electric razor he flipped on the switch and began to shave. And he wasn't going to sink, either.

He was sinking faster than the *Titanic,* Jacques admitted twenty minutes later as he followed Liza into the living room. She placed her overnight bag beside the door, and when she turned around, he blocked her path. "What do you mean, you are leaving?"

Liza tipped her chin up. The smile she gave him was as bright and phony as a cubic zirconia. "Just what I said. I'm going home."

"Just like that?"

"Yes," she said calmly. "Is there some reason I shouldn't go?"

"Yes. No." Panic seized him, and along with it came anger. "What about last night?"

"Well, the gala was a tremendous success, in large part due to you. I don't know how to tha—"

"I am not talking about the damn gala!" He grabbed her shoulders, furious with her and himself. "I am talking about *us.* You and me. And what went on between us in that bedroom last night."

"Last night was…well, it was wonderful, Jacques. I don't have to tell you that you're a very skilled lover. You already know it." Color climbed up her cheeks, but her gaze didn't waver. "Last night was very special to me. I'll cherish the memory of it always."

"That's it?" Enraged, he wanted to shake her. He released her instead. He raked his hands through his hair and paced the length of the room. It was happening too fast, too soon. He wanted more time. He'd counted on having more time. He wasn't ready to let her go just yet. He whipped around and glared at her. "You plan to just waltz right out of here with a 'Thanks for a good time, but so long'?"

"I think it's for the best. I know what your feelings are on commitment, and I think you know mine. We're both adults, Jacques. I don't see any point in drawing this thing out and pretending there was more to last night than there was."

Temper took him by storm, bathing her and everything in his vision in a red mist. "And just what *was* last night to you, Liza?"

"It...it was a wonderful interlude for me. Just as I hope it was for you. But it's over. And I think it's better if we end things now. I know your feelings about not wanting anyone to get in too deep."

Jacques felt himself go under for the third time. Unable to stop himself, he marched over to Liza and hauled her up against him. "Well, it is too late. I am already in too deep." He kissed her, then. It was an angry, punishing kiss, filled with all the fury and fear inside him.

She struggled against him, wrestled to free her wrists from his grasp. He tightened his hold. At the sound of her whimper, Jacques released her immediately. Guilt raced through him at the thought that he had hurt her. He started to lift his head. "Liza, I—"

She curled her fingers into his shirt and pressed her mouth against his, cutting off the apology he'd been about to make. Gently, sweetly, she soothed him with her lips. When she released him and he lifted his head, she asked, "Now what was that you said about being in too deep?"

Oh, Lord, what had he said? He stepped away from her,

scrubbed his hand over his face. "I said I am already in too deep." And he was, Jacques realized. He was in deeper than he'd ever dreamed he could be.

"Exactly what does that mean?"

What did it mean? He didn't know what it meant. Didn't want to think about what it meant.

"Jacques? Are you saying that you love me?"

"No!" Just the word alone had panic racing through him. A cold sweat broke out across his brow.

"Then what?"

"How the hell do I know what it means?" He was furious with himself for feeling; furious with her for making him feel. He could tell by the look in her eyes that she wanted more than he was willing to give her. But he couldn't bring himself to just walk away from her. "It means...it means I do not think I will ever be able to give you what you want. In fact, I am sure I cannot. But I...I cannot just let you walk out of my life the way you did the last time."

Liza stared at him for long moments. "So what do you suggest we do?"

"How the hell do I know?" He raked his hands through his hair, growing more irritated by the second that she could stand there looking so cool, so calm, when inside he was dying. Didn't she know how hard this was for him? He'd sworn never to allow himself to feel this way about anyone. He'd sworn never to run the risk of wanting what he knew he couldn't have.

"Well, if you figure out just what it is you want, you know how to reach me." She reached for her bag.

"Wait!"

Liza set her case back down and turned to him again. He drew in a deep breath. "What if—" He swallowed. "Maybe we could try living together for a while."

"You want me to live with you?"

"Yes." Oh, Lord, he couldn't believe he'd said it.

"Maybe if we lived together for a while we could see if this...this thing that is between us, if it is strong enough to last or if it will just burn itself out."

Feeling a bit unsteady, he sank down on the nearest chair. After his head cleared, he realized Liza hadn't responded. He looked up to find her studying him with dark, somber eyes. For the life of him, he couldn't make out what she was thinking, and that had his stomach knotting up again. "So what do you think? Do we make an attempt at living together?"

"I need some time to think about it."

"Fine. Take your time," he told her, not sure if he was relieved or not.

"But before I give you my answer, there's someone I'd like you to meet."

She probably wanted him to meet her brother. What was his name? Edward. Yes, that was it. Edward. She'd told him the guy he'd seen her with at the children's center had been her brother. Feeling somewhat better, he said, "Sure. But I thought you said your brother and his family already left."

"They did."

Puzzled, he asked, "Then who is it you want me to meet?"

"Jack."

Dear God, please don't let this be a mistake, Liza prayed as she checked in her rearview mirror to make sure Jacques had followed her off the highway exit marked St. Charles. She had been all set to walk away that morning, to never see him again and get on with her life.

And then he'd suggested they try living together. For a man who shunned commitment, it was a major turnabout. Liza shook her head in wonder. She wasn't sure who had been more surprised by the offer, her or Jacques.

She bit back a grin, remembering the shock on his face,

how deathly pale he had gone after he'd realized what he'd said. She could never remember seeing him so distraught, so unsure of himself. Heaven help her, but she'd decided to take a chance and tell him the truth.

Flipping on the turn signal, Liza drove onto the street leading to her home. Snow-covered trees, lined up like sentinels, stretched down the length of the street. Christmas tree lights winked from behind windows, reminding her it was only a few days until Christmas. As she turned into the driveway of her brick and stucco ranch house, the big green wreath with its bright red bow and bells brought a smile to her lips. Please, please for all of our sakes, but especially for Jack's, don't let this have been a mistake.

After pulling her car into the garage, Liza retrieved her bag from the trunk and waited at the doorway for Jacques to park his car and join her. Judging from the scowl on his face as he exited his vehicle, he was no happier now than he had been an hour earlier when she'd refused to answer any of his questions about Jack and had insisted they drive separately.

The separate cars had been a defense measure on her part, Liza admitted. She hadn't wanted to be interrogated by Jacques during the drive, but more important, she had wanted him to have a means of escape if he decided he wanted no part of her and his son.

Her stomach did a nervous little jig as she thought about his reaction to discovering he was a father. But before she could dwell on it further Jacques stormed his way across the snow-covered lawn to her side. "All right, Liza. I am here. Now what kind of game is it you are playing?"

A gust of wind sent flakes of snow scurrying across the yard and Liza's hair dancing into her eyes. She brushed the strands away from her face and dug out her key. "It's no game, Jacques." She shoved the key into the lock and pushed the door open.

Jacques followed her inside. "No?" He caught her arm

and turned her to face him as soon as the door closed. "You wanted to make me jealous, didn't you? Well, you have succeeded," he spat out before she could tell him he was wrong. "And if you wanted to find out if I wanted you enough to fight for you, then the answer is 'Yes, I do.' You are mine, Liza. And I will fight your Jack or anyone else I have to."

Liza caught his hand, pressed his fingers to her lips. There was anger in this man she'd lost her heart to and there was violence. She could feel it radiating through him like waves. But there was also fear in him. It was the fear that tore at her heartstrings. "I'm not a prize up for grabs, Jacques. I don't want you to fight for me. You don't have to. I love you. I always have. And I want to be with you."

"And I want you, *chérie*." He started to pull her into his arms. I—"

Not love, want. Beating back her disappointment, Liza stepped out of his embrace and lifted her gaze to meet his. "The question is will you still want me after I tell you the real reason I left you three years ago."

"Mommy!"

Liza spun around at the sound of her son's voice. She smiled and dropped to her knees in time to catch the blond-haired bundle of energy hurling himself toward her on little legs. "Hi, baby." She kissed his head and hugged him close, breathing in the scent of baby, crayons and chocolate chip cookies. When he began squirming in her arms, she reluctantly released him and stood.

"Who him?" Jack asked, looking up at Jacques out of curious gold eyes.

Bracing herself, Liza turned towards Jacques. Her heart stopped, or at least it seemed to. She rubbed the spot on her chest to assure herself her heart still worked. It did. And any minute now she was sure it would break into tiny pieces.

Jacques's face had turned the color of chalk. His body

could have been made of stone it was so still—except for his eyes. They moved from Jack to her and back again, blazing with emotion, reminding her of the white-hot gold of flames.

"Who him, Mommy?" Jack persisted.

Pulling herself together, Liza took her son's hand. "This is..." She swallowed. "This is Mr. Gaston. He's a...a friend of Mommy's. Jacques, this is Jack. My son."

"I make cookies," Jack told him, holding up the half-eaten chocolate chip in his hand. He took a step toward Jacques. "Taste?"

For long seconds Jacques didn't move, didn't say anything, and when he stooped down to take a bite, the knot in Liza's stomach twisted a little tighter.

"Jack, you little rascal, where are you?"

At the sound of Mrs. Murphy's voice, Liza released a breath she hadn't even realized she'd been holding.

"I here." Jack turned and ran laughing into the arms of his sitter.

The apple-cheeked woman gathered him into her arms and hugged him to her with affectionate ease. "I thought I heard you come in, Liza, but I had to get that batch of gingerbread men out of the oven." Releasing Jack she wiped her hands on her apron.

"No problem. Mrs. Murphy, this is Mr. Gaston. He's a friend of mine."

"How do you do?" the other woman said, nodding. From the way she eyed him and little Jack, Liza suspected she recognized the resemblance and the connection. "And you, you little scamp," she told Jack. "You swiped another cookie, didn't you?"

"For him." Jack pointed to Jacques.

"Is that so?" Mrs. Murphy asked. She arched her brow and looked over at Jacques who had yet to move from inside the doorway.

Jack nodded. "Him wanted," Jack insisted, then ran over

to Jacques and grabbed him around the legs. "Him wanted."

Liza's heart seemed to lodge itself in her throat at the sight of her son, clinging to his father's legs. And from his utterly stunned expression and the stiffness of his body, Jacques had no idea what to do with the child. "Jack, let Mr. Gaston go and come to Mommy, sweetheart."

"No," her son said and clung tighter to Jacques.

"Jack," Liza admonished and made a move to retrieve her son.

"It's all right, Liza," Jacques said, surprising her. His fingers lightly brushed her son's head. "The cookie was very good, Mrs. Murphy. I've never tasted better."

The elderly woman flushed under his praise. "Well, there's plenty more in the kitchen if you'd like to have some. I'll put on a pot of coffee for you and your guest," she told Liza. "Come on, Jack. You can help me."

But instead of going to Mrs. Murphy as he usually would, Jack stretched his arms up to Jacques. "Up," he demanded.

Liza's hands clenched into tight fists at her sides as she noted Jacques's hesitation. If he rejected her son, she would die, she thought—right after she murdered Jacques.

"Up," Jack insisted, tugging on Jacques's pants leg with chocolate fingers and holding out his arms again.

"Let me take off my coat first, okay?"

"'Kay."

Liza breathed a sigh of relief. "I know we have to talk, Jacques. I'm sure you have some questions," she said, taking his coat from him.

He leveled her with a look that was filled with frustration, anger, fear. But before he could say anything, Jack was tugging at his pants leg again.

This was Jack? This was the Jack he'd been hating, wanting to tear limb from limb? Jacques looked down at the boy, noting the pale blond hair so like Liza's. The mouth, the cheekbones and the nose were similar, smaller versions of his own. But it was the eyes—his eyes—that stared up at him.

"Up," Jack demanded again.

Reaching down, Jacques lifted him into his arms. The little arms circled his neck. A sharp ache sliced through his chest. A son. He had a son.

"The kitchen's this way," Liza said.

Jacques followed her through the house, vaguely aware of his surroundings, far too conscious of the tiny being he held in his arms.

"Mrs. Murphy, will you join us for some coffee?" Liza asked.

"Thank you, dear. But I need to be getting home."

"What about your cookies?" Liza asked.

"Oh, they're for you and Jack. But you'll have to frost that last batch yourself. I didn't realize how late it was. My daughter, Millie, and her children are coming to pick me up this evening, and I still need to pack. I'll be spending the holiday with them."

"Then you won't be here for Christmas."

"No. But I'll be back after the New Year."

"Well, thank you for taking care of Jack. I hope he wasn't too much trouble."

"Not at all," Mrs. Murphy assured her. "He's a charmer that one."

Liza slanted him a glance. "Jack, come give Mrs. Murphy a goodbye kiss."

"Leave him be. He's quite happy where he is." The other woman waved her away. She walked over and kissed Jack's cheek. "Nice to meet you, Mr. Gaston."

"My pleasure," Jacques replied. He didn't miss the way Mrs. Murphy's brown eyes moved from Jack to him.

"I'll walk you out. I have a little something under the tree for you," Liza said.

Fighting through the swirl of emotions going through him, Jacques stood in the middle of the kitchen. His artist's eye swept over the room. It was small compared to the one in the Gallaghers' apartment, but it was welcoming and reflected Liza's good taste. The walls were covered in a leaf green and lemon print. The scent of chocolate chip cookies and ginger and spice filled every corner. But it was the mixture of winter sunshine, baby powder and crayons that registered.

He looked at the boy he held in his arms, noted the crayons poking out of the pocket of his navy corduroys. Jacques grinned as he glanced at the refrigerator, the white surface was barely visible beneath the slew of magnets holding up a child's drawings. Another artist, he thought bemused, then stopped with a jolt. Not just any artist, his son.

A lump rose in Jacques's throat. He swallowed. These were not just any child's drawings, they were *his son's* drawings. *His* son had made the scribblings displayed as refrigerator art. Jacques's chest swelled with a sense of wonder and pride. He had a son. He and Liza had created this beautiful little boy.

And by creating a son, the legacy of Gaston would live on. Panic whipped through him again as he stared at the child. Maybe he was wrong. Maybe the boy wasn't his.

"Want cookie," Jack informed him and pointed to a rack of gingerbread men cooling on a Formica countertop next to the oven. Colored sprinkles and bowls of red and green frosting sat a few feet away. A Santa cookie jar and two heaping plates of cookies cluttered the adjacent counter.

Jacques walked over to the plates of iced gingerbread men and chocolate chips, with Jack in his arms. "Which one?" he asked.

The boy looked at him, his green eyes twinkled. "Want bofe." Before Jack could stop him, he reached out with both hands and snagged one of each. He smiled at Jacques and bit off the gingerbread man's head.

Jacques couldn't help himself, he laughed. "Good?"

He nodded and held the decapitated cookie up for Jacques to take a bite. He bit off a piece and laughed again. "You are right. It is good."

"How would you like some coffee to go with that?" Liza asked from the doorway. She directed him to the table and chairs positioned in front of the expanse of windows that dominated the room. White gauzy curtains pulled back with lemon-colored sashes allowed sunshine to gleam through the window. Jacques glanced out at the snow-covered backyard, noting the jungle gym and child's swing.

"Have a seat, Jacques," Liza said as she placed a plate of cookies on the table. She held out her arms. "Come to Mommy, sweetheart. You can sit in your chair, and I'll get you some milk."

Jack licked the last of the icing off the gingerbread man, ending up with more on his face and shirt than his mouth. He reached over to snag another one from the plate.

Liza grabbed his hand. "Oh no you don't, young man. Finish your milk. It's almost time for your nap."

"Please, Mommy. One more cookie?" he asked.

Jacques's stomach did a nosedive as he watched the boy flash his mother a grin—a grin that he recognized as a version of his own.

"All right. One more cookie and then it's time for your nap."

One cookie and thirty minutes later, Jacques paced the living room while he waited for Liza to finish putting Jack down for his nap. He looked at the Christmas tree, covered in white lights and shiny ornaments, its tip crowned with a bright red star that bent slightly at the ceiling. His thoughts drifted back to that Christmas three years ago. He had revealed so much of himself to her back then. He'd trusted her, had told her about his father and the darkness he carried inside him. There was never supposed to be a child. He'd sworn he would not sire another Gaston to carry on that seed of darkness. But Liza had betrayed him. Because of her, he had broken his own vow and his father had won.

Angry, Jacques whipped around and spotted her standing in the doorway watching him. "I do not suppose that there is a chance he is not mine?" he asked, making no attempt to mask the anger or coldness inside him.

He caught the slight wince before she could stop it. "He's yours, Jacques. If you choose not to believe me, then that's your decision."

"There is always a paternity test."

She hiked up her chin in that way that only she could pull off and walked regally over to the fireplace. She picked up the poker to shift a log. "I don't need a paternity test, Jacques. In the four years since my divorce, I've only slept with one person. And that person was you."

Her words cut him and made him even angrier. "Unlike me. Is that what you are saying? That I have slept with many women? Used them?"

"Only you can answer that," she said coolly.

It was the coolness that ate at him, fed his anger. Because there had been other women since she'd left him, although not nearly as many as she might think, and he realized he had used them all in his attempt to forget her. Only he hadn't forgotten her, would never forget her. "Why did you not tell me?" he demanded, bitter when he thought of all those weeks, months, years he had spent hating her, wanting her. And heaven help him, even now, knowing what she had done, he still wanted her. "Why did you not tell me?" he repeated, grabbing her arm and causing the poker to fall from her fingers to the hearth.

"I tried to tell you. That last night we were together, I planned to. But when I brought up the subject of children, you told me you didn't want any. That you never planned to marry or have a family."

"And I told you the reason why," he reminded her. "I told you about the vow I made to myself to never father a child. I thought you understood. You said you accepted it."

"What choice did I have?"

"You could have made sure you did not get pregnant or had me use protection."

"It was too late. I was already pregnant," she argued.

"If you had told me the truth that night, we could have taken care of it."

"No," Liza said, her voice a horrified whisper, her face as white as a sheet. When she started to pull away, he tightened his grip on her wrist and forced her to look at him.

"I trusted you." He spit out the words, anger ripping him apart inside. "I trusted you when you told me you were protected, but you lied to me, Liza. And you lied to me again by not telling me you were pregnant."

"Jacques, you're hurting me."

He saw fear flicker in her eyes, heard it in her voice. It only inflamed him more. "Hurt? You do not know the meaning of hurt. I *hurt,* Liza. I hurt because you made me love you three years ago and left me. I hurt because you gave me a son I never wanted. I hurt because you made me love you again now, when I know I can never have you."

"Jacques, please. Let me go."

She had given him a taste, a glimpse of everything he wanted but could never have. And he hated her for letting him know all that he would be missing.

"Jacques, please. You're hurting me."

Slowly Liza's words penetrated through the fog of his anger. He saw the fear in her eyes and stared down at her wrist clutched tightly in his fist. Then he saw the red marks on her pale skin as she struggled to break free.

Appalled, he released her at once and looked at his hands. Big hands. Strong hands, he thought. Hands like his father's. And he'd used them to hurt Liza. Horrified by his actions, that he had used his strength to hurt her, Jacques jerked away from her. He sank down in a chair, buried his head in his hands. He felt ill. Worse, he realized his father's prophecy had come true. He *was* just like his father. The darkness *was* there inside him just as the old man had said, just as he had always feared. And he'd used that darkness against Liza.

"Jacques." Liza knelt beside him, pulled his hands away from his face. "Please, look at me. I didn't lie to you. I swear I didn't. I didn't think I could get pregnant. I—I'd tried for years during my marriage and couldn't. I had this thing they call endometriosis. I'd already lost one ovary and been told that the other one was infected. I thought I was going to have to have a hysterectomy."

Tears streamed down her face as she continued, but all Jacques could do was look at the red marks on her wrist. "When I found out I was pregnant, it…it was a miracle. I tried to tell you…that last night we were together. But then you told me about your father."

Jacques looked at her then, her eyes bright and pleading, her beautiful face stained with tears. Tears that he had caused. A chill settled over him. "Did I tell you what a cruel, ill-tempered man Etienne Gaston was, Liza? He was, you know. He had a vicious temper. And big fists. Big fists like these." He held up his own fists to show her. "And did I tell you about the darkness in him that had him use those fists on my mother? On me? But he was good-looking and charming. The ladies loved him. My mother loved him so much that she refused to leave him. No matter what he did to her, no matter how many times he was unfaithful to her or cruel to her or to me. She stayed with him until living with him killed her."

"You're not your father, Jacques."

"I am my father's son. I have his face. His hands. Hands

that hurt you just now. That might hurt you again. I am Etienne Gaston's son. I carry his seed of darkness in me.''

"There is no darkness in you, Jacques," she insisted. "You're not cruel like your father. You would never deliberately hurt anyone."

"No?" He looked at her. "I was ready to kill Jack when I thought he was another man." He took her wrist, rubbed his fingers across the red marks, knowing tomorrow there would be bruises. It sickened him that he had been the instrument of such pain. "And what do you call this? I hurt you. I *wanted* to hurt you. Do not tell me there is no darkness in me. It is there, Liza. I feel it inside me. I see it, even if you do not."

Liza grabbed his hands, gathered them to her. "Listen to me, Jacques. There is no such thing as a bad seed. And even if there was, even if you did get a...a bad temper from your father, what about the things you got from your mother? You told me she was kind and gentle. You said she was an artist. Isn't she the one you credit for your talent?"

Jacques stared at their joined hands and looked into her eyes, shimmering with tears, as she continued. "You...me, everyone is more than our genetic makeup. We're more than the composite of whose blood runs through our veins. Each of us is responsible for what we make of ourselves, for what we feel in our hearts. So are you, Jacques. So are you."

How he wanted to believe her, wished that he could. He looked at the ugly marks on her wrists and knew it was a lie. "But the darkness is a part of me, too, Liza. I cannot escape it."

Liza's heart pounded in her chest as he stood and went to retrieve his coat. "I will be leaving Chicago day after tomorrow."

"What about us? You asked me to live with you. Why does our having a son together change everything?"

"I realize now I was only kidding myself. It would never have worked, Liza. Even if Jack did not exist. You want children, a family. I cannot give them to you."

"What about Jack? You have a son, Jacques. Whether you want him or not. He's still your son."

"I am aware of that. I will send you money for him, but I do not wish him to know me as his father. I do not wish to be a part of his life."

"That's it? You're just going to walk out of here and pretend he doesn't exist? That I no longer exist?"

"It is better this way."

"For who?" Liza demanded.

He slipped on his coat. He walked over to her, brushed the tears away from her cheeks. "For you and for Jack."

Liza wrenched away from him, hugged her arms around herself, trying to stop the pain. "You said you loved me. If you love me, Jacques, prove it. Stay. Make a life with me and our son. I need you. Our son needs you. He needs a father."

There was pain there, there was longing. She saw it in his face, in his eyes. But Liza was too caught up in her own agony to offer comfort.

"You made the right decision years ago, Liza. Jack is better off with no father than to have me as one. You are better off without me, too. I love you. Too much to risk hurting you again because of the darkness in me. Enough to walk away and let you find someone else who will make you happy."

He opened the door, and a rush of cold air came in, setting the flames to dance in the fireplace. But Liza could feel no cold. All she could feel was the pain in her heart.

"I once accused you of being a gigolo, Jacques, because of your aversion to commitment. I was wrong. Even a gigolo's willing to take a chance on love. You're not. You're a coward, Jacques Gaston. You're so afraid your father was right, that you're not willing to take a chance—not even on my love for you or for our son. And you know what's so ironic about all of this?''

Wiping away the tears running down her cheeks, she continued, ''What's so ironic, is that by not taking that chance, you let your father win. He wins, Jacques. He wins because you're going to end up just like him. Alone.''

Eleven

"**D**o you hear me, Jacques? He wins," Liza sobbed. "Your father wins after all!"

Jacques forced himself to turn away, forced himself to walk down the sidewalk toward his car. The snow continued to fall, harder now, the wind whipping it around him and into his eyes. It was cold. He knew it was cold. It had to be, given the strength of the wind. But he didn't feel it. He didn't feel the bite of the wind or the sting of snow. He couldn't feel anything except the deep, numbing ache inside him.

"You're a coward, Jacques Gaston. You're a coward for letting him win."

He kept moving toward the car, afraid if he stopped or looked back for even a moment, he wouldn't be able to leave. Opening the car door, he slipped behind the wheel and started the engine. He didn't bother with the seat belt. He didn't care about his own safety. He simply had to leave—quickly, before he lost the courage to walk away

from her and his son, away from the only things in life that
he wanted. The very things he could never have.

Leave. Don't look.

He obeyed the voice in his head. Shoving the gearshift
into reverse, he backed the car out of the driveway and set
the tires spinning on the ice-packed driveway.

Go quickly. Don't look at her.

He heard the voice in his head and knew he should listen,
but as he braked the car, slowing on the downward slope
of the driveway to the icy street, he couldn't stop himself.
He had to see her, to look at her one last time.

She stood in the doorway, a vision in her dark green
slacks and matching turtleneck with her chin hiked up
proudly, defiantly, her hair a swirl of blond silk thrashing
in the wind and snow. He saw her turn, crouch down and
scoop Jack up as the boy ran into her arms.

Then Jack waved to him. His son waved his little fingers.
Pain ripped through him again, and Jacques wrenched his
gaze away. His vision blurred. He could no longer see the
road clearly, but he had to go...quickly. Before he could
change his mind, he took his foot off the brake and, shifting
the car into first gear, he hit the gas. The Mercedes sedan
shot down the street into the blur of white snow. He pressed
the heel of his hand to one eye, then to the other and somehow navigated his way along the winding road.

But even as he followed the road signs directing him
back to Chicago, he couldn't shake the image of Liza and
Jack standing in the doorway watching him leave.

And an hour later as he exited the elevator and headed
to the penthouse apartment, he could still hear Liza's words
ringing in his ears.

*"He wins, Jacques. Your father wins because you're go-
ing to end up just like him."*

She was wrong, Jacques told himself. He'd done the right
thing—for Liza and their son. If he had stayed as she'd
asked him to do, as he had wanted to do, then his father

really would have won. Because by staying he would have
exposed them to the darkness inside him. He thought of the
way Liza had looked when he left her, her beautiful face
all tear streaked, her eyes swollen from crying. The ugly
marks on her wrists. Marks that *he* had made in anger.

No, Jacques told himself once more. He had defeated
Etienne Gaston. The cycle would end with him, just as he
had vowed it would. Liza and Jack were free. They could
make a new life without him, a life not touched by his
darkness.

Inserting his key into the lock of the apartment, Jacques
stepped inside the living room. Silence greeted him. Silence
and emptiness.

Tossing his overcoat on a chair, he headed for the bar
and poured himself a glass of bourbon. As he lifted the
glass to his lips, Jacques caught a glimpse of himself in the
mirror behind the bar. His hair was damp with melted snow
and looked as though he hadn't combed it in days. A five
o'clock shadow covered his chin and jaw, evidence that he
hadn't shaved since morning. But it was his eyes, so empty
and old that startled him. With the glass in his hands, the
opened bottle before him and those empty gold eyes, he
saw his father again. It was his father staring back at him.
Slowly Jacques put down the glass and scrubbed his hand
over his face.

Sleep. What he needed was sleep, Jacques told himself.
Turning away from the bar, he headed for the bedroom. He
didn't bother with the lights, simply kicked of his shoes
and threw his clothes on a chair before falling facedown
on the bed.

Gardenias.

The smell surrounded him. Jacques groaned. He fisted
his hands in the sheets. He was enveloped in the smell of
gardenias and Liza. And with the scents came flashes of
the previous night that he had spent here with Liza in his
arms, her body wrapped around his.

Flipping over onto his back, he brought his arm across his eyes. Dear God, how was he going to live without her, he wondered, as he tried to shut out the images of her. But as he drifted off into a fitful sleep, he could still see her face as she'd looked in the doorway, and he could still hear her words ringing over and over in his head.

It was to the sound of Aimee Gallagher's voice on the answering machine in the next room that he awoke the next morning. "Jacques? Jacques, it's Aimee. If you're there, please pick up."

Jacques squinted at the clock that read eleven-fifteen and realized that he'd slept through the night and most of the morning.

"Jacques, are you there?"

He scrambled for the portable phone on the bedside table, managing to knock it on the floor before grabbing the receiver. "Aimee. I am here, *mon amie.*"

"Jacques, what in the world is going on?"

"What do you mean?"

"I spoke with Liza this morning and she sounded awful. She said...I know she told you about Jack. But she said you'd left. That you...that you didn't want them."

Jacques squeezed his eyes shut a moment. "Aimee, I know you mean well, and I appreciate it. But please, stay out of this. It is between Liza and me."

"Is it true then? Are you really just going to walk away from them? I thought you loved her, Jacques."

"I *do* love her." And the pain of loving her and being forced to turn away from what he wanted hit him again like a blow.

"Then how can you just walk away? I thought—"

"Aimee, please. Leave it alone. I have to go. I need to pack."

"Wait, Jacques. Don't hang up."

Jacques sighed. Getting up from the bed, he wandered to

the studio he had been using to work in. "What do you want, Aimee?"

"You said you had to pack."

"That is right. It is time that I leave. The gala is over, and my lecture series ended last week."

"But where are you going?"

He wasn't at all sure. He only knew that he had to get away. "I am thinking about taking a little vacation to someplace in the Caribbean." He picked up one of the brochures lying on the table. He had gathered a handful from a travel agency the previous week. He'd known a week ago that he would need to get away after the gala was over in order to forget Liza. Then yesterday morning, after their passion-filled night together, he had decided to surprise Liza by sweeping her away for a trip. As it was he would be taking the trip after all—but without Liza. "After all of this snow, I find myself in the mood for some sun and sand."

"But what about Christmas?"

"What about it?" Jacques asked.

"Tomorrow's Christmas Eve. Surely you're not planning to spend Christmas on some island with a bunch of strangers," Aimee replied, as though the idea of tropical breezes and warm sunshine were repugnant.

"Aimee, *mon amie*, when have you ever known me to remain a stranger for long?"

"Stop the charming-Frenchman act, Jacques," she chided, obviously not buying his attempt to lighten the conversation and her worries. "Christmas is a time for families, and if you're not going to spend it with Liza and your son, then you're going to spend it with us."

"Aimee, I appreciate—"

"I'm not taking no for an answer, Jacques Gaston. And neither will Peter. We'll have tickets delivered to the apartment this evening, so you have time to finish anything you have to do there. Tomorrow you'll come to New Orleans and spend the holiday with us."

And before he could argue further, the line went dead.
Jacques stared at the phone in his hands for long seconds.
Maybe New Orleans wouldn't be such a bad place to spend
Christmas, after all, Jacques decided. Right now anyplace
was better than being trapped in this city and apartment
with so many memories of Liza and knowing that she was
so near, but forever beyond his reach.

But as he packed his clothes and his art equipment,
Jacques found no peace in his decision to leave. When he
started to pack the finished bust he had done of Aimee and
Peter's daughter, to take to them as a Christmas gift, he
kept seeing the image of Jack.

Jack would make a great subject, he thought, and was
shocked at how strong his desire was to do a similar bust
of his son. *His son.* Jacques swallowed the lump in his
throat. He would never have the opportunity to sketch the
little boy's face, capture that twinkle in his eye on canvas,
recreate that baby smile in clay.

Jacques squeezed his eyes shut to turn off the images of
Jack demanding to be picked up, of Jack laughing, of tiny
hands grabbing cookies. Behind his shuttered lids he saw
a fistful of crayons sticking out of a little boy's pockets, a
refrigerator almost invisible beneath a child's drawings, a
small boy tucked in his mother's arms at a doorway waving
his little hand in goodbye.

*"He wins, Jacques. Your father wins because you're go-
ing to end up just like him. Alone."*

And he was alone, Jacques admitted. Just as his father
had been in the end. But it had been *his* decision, Jacques
told himself. He'd made the right choice for Liza and their
son. He tried to dredge up memories of his father, of his
cruelties, of his laughing smirk when he'd told Jacques that
he was just like him. But all he could see was Liza's face,
hear Liza's voice pleading with him to stay.

"I love you, Jacques. Stay. Don't go."

Jacques covered his ears with his hands, but he couldn't escape her tearful voice.

"We're more than the composite of whose blood runs through our veins. Each of us is responsible for what we make of ourselves, for what we feel in our heart. So are you, Jacques. So are you."

Had Liza been right? By walking away, had he let his father win? His heart beat faster as Jacques thought about what was in his heart. In his heart there was love—for Liza and the child that they had created out of that love.

He struggled to find the darkness inside him. But he couldn't, not when he imagined Liza's face, the way she had looked when she had offered him her body and told him she loved him. There was no darkness when he thought of her, so soft and loving as she held their son. And there was no darkness when he remembered Jack's laughter or the feel of his arms circling his neck.

No. There was no darkness in his heart now, not when he thought of Liza or their son. He was still Etienne Gaston's son, Jacques admitted. It was still his father's blood that ran through his veins. It was still his father's face and vicious temper he possessed. But his heart, his heart was his own, and it was filled with love for Liza and their son.

"Christmas is a time for families."

Aimee was right. Christmas *was* a time for families. And he had a family to spend this Christmas with—his own. But first, he had some shopping to do.

"No, Mother. I'm sure. I really want Jack and me to spend Christmas in our own home. Yes. I promise. Jack and I will drive up the day after Christmas to see you and Dad. I love you, too. Goodbye," Liza told her mother.

She returned the telephone to its cradle and, pasting a smile on her lips, she turned to Jack. "Okay. Now I wonder who is going to help Mommy frost these cookies?"

"I help," Jack offered.

Liza looked at her son, so like his father, and felt that fist squeezing her heart again. She scooped him up into her arms and hugged him to her. After all the crying she'd done the previous night, she had been sure she didn't have another tear inside her to shed. She was wrong, Liza realized, as silent tears ran down her cheeks.

Despite her own pain, she thought of the way Jacques had looked when he'd left her. So terribly, terribly alone. Poor Jacques. At least she had their son, Liza told herself, and she found her heart hurting for Jacques who had no one.

Trying to pull herself together, Liza reminded herself that thanks to Aimee, Jacques wouldn't be spending the Christmas holiday alone. *Oh, Jacques. You should be here—with me and our son.*

Jack squirmed in her arms and Liza eased her hold. His little fingers touched the tears on her cheek. ''Hurt?'' he asked.

''Yes, sweetie, it hurts,'' Liza admitted. And it did hurt to know that Jacques loved her, but not enough.

''I kiss. Make better.''

And when he kissed her cheek, Liza hugged him closer and told herself it would be all right. After all, she still had her son. Pulling herself together, Liza swiped the tears from her cheeks. ''Okay, let's get these cookies frosted,'' she told him.

After setting Jack down in a chair, she placed a small tray of the sugar cookies that had been cut into Santa Claus faces and teddy bear shapes. Then she and Jack dipped their brushes into the bowls of red and white frosting. ''Now which ones do you want us to leave out tonight for Santa Claus?''

''Bear,'' he told her and began to paint.

As Liza oohed and ahhed over her son's masterpieces she found herself watching the clock and thinking of Jacques again. After her second conversation with Aimee yesterday in which she learned that Jacques had accepted her invitation to spend Christmas in New Orleans, she'd been keenly aware of the day as it related to Jacques.

At nine o'clock that morning, she had imagined him packing his bags. At ten o'clock, she envisioned him turning in his rental car. When eleven-thirty arrived and she thought of him boarding the plane for New Orleans, Liza could feel the tears welling up inside her again.

Suddenly she had to get out of the house, away from the clock and the mental images of Jacques's leaving. "Sweetheart, how would you like to help Mommy build a snowman?" she asked her son.

"Make 'noman." He held out his arms.

Liza hurriedly bundled Jack up in his coat, hat and mittens. Not bothering to take the time with a hat for herself, she threw on her coat and gloves and raced out of the door into the snow and sunshine.

As she began helping Jack pack the snow into a small mound, she found herself glancing up at the sky. She was being ridiculous, Liza told herself. They were too far from the airport for her to see or hear the planes take off. Still, she found herself shielding her eyes from the sun and watching the sky as her mental itinerary of Jacques's movements continued. She envisioned him getting on the plane, buckling his seat belt, smiling and making some lucky stewardess's day when he flirted with her.

She was so lost in her thoughts, that at first Liza didn't see the familiar dark Mercedes turn the corner onto her street. Her pulse quickened when she saw the car, and for a moment she thought it was Jacques.

He's gone, Liza. Accept it and get on with your life. You still have Jack, she reminded herself. Chastising herself, she dusted the snow off her hands and walked over to her son. "Hey, tiger, what do you say we take a break for lunch?"

"Make 'noman," he told her and continued to pound the snow.

"We can have peanut butter and jelly sandwiches."

"And cookies?"

"And cookies, you little rascal," she agreed. Laughing, she pulled him to his feet, dusted off the snow from his pants and swung him up into her arms.

She had no sooner freed Jack of his mittens, hat and coat and got him quieted in the kitchen when the doorbell rang. "Be right there," she called out.

When Jack started to get up and race for the door. Liza caught him instead. "Oh, no you don't, buster. Mommy will answer it. You stay here and finish your milk. I'll be right back."

Satisfied that her son would stay put, Liza hurried to the front of the house and pulled open the door. Her heart stopped, then started again.

Jacques stood in the doorway, his arms overflowing with brightly wrapped packages, a Santa Claus hat on his head. But it was his eyes, golden and bright, filled with hesitation and hope, that kept Liza riveted and her tongue glued to the roof of her mouth. She couldn't believe he was here, that she wasn't imagining him standing there.

"Say something, Liza," he said, and she realized the hesitation she'd detected in his eyes was because of her.

"I didn't think you would come back," she finally managed to say.

"I could not stay away. I do not want to be alone anymore, Liza. I do not want to be the man my father was. And I do not want my life to end as his did—alone and in darkness. With no love or light in my life."

"What is it you want from me, Jacques?" she asked, her heart thundering with hope.

"I had a good friend remind me that Christmas is a time for families. *You* are my family, Liza. You and Jack. I love you. I am hoping it is not too late. That you will give me a chance to prove it to both of you."

"What about the darkness, Jacques? What about the bad seed you believe is inside you?"

"It is still there. I suspect it will always be there inside me. Just as I suspect I will always have the dark temper. But I know now that there is also light inside me, in my heart. You and Jack are my light, Liza. I am not afraid to fight the darkness—not as long as I have you and your love to help me. Do you...can you possibly still love me?"

"Oh, Jacques. I've always loved you. I always will."

Jacques dropped the packages onto the floor and opened his arms. Liza went into them, and when he kissed her, her heart nearly burst with joy.

"There is a package here," Jacques told her between kisses. Not letting her go, he stooped down and rummaged through the bright boxes. He picked out a small one in silver paper with a beautiful red bow. He handed it to Liza.

"But it's not Christmas yet," she protested.

"I know, but open it, anyway."

With trembling fingers Liza ripped open the package and stared at the ring. An emerald-cut diamond, set in a band of gold.

"It is an engagement ring. I have the wedding band that matches it in my pocket. I love you, Liza. Please say you will marry me."

Liza threw her arms around his neck again.

"Is that a yes?" he asked, but his mouth was already curving in a wicked smile.

"You know it is." Holding out her hand, she allowed Jacques to slip the ring on her finger and then kissed him again.

"Santa Claus!" Jack exclaimed from the doorway. His eyes were wide, his little mouth agape.

Liza looked from her son to Jacques and burst into laughter at his shocked expression. Oh, life was good, and this Christmas was going to be such a beautiful one, she thought.

Jack rushed over to Jacques as quickly as his little legs would take him. He tugged on his father's pants leg. "Up, up," he demanded.

And as Jacques lifted their son into his arms, Liza knew that Jacques had beaten the darkness. There could never be darkness as long as there was love.

*   *   *   *   *

Silhouette's newest series

YOURS TRULY

Love when you least expect it.

Where the written word plays a vital role in uniting couples—you're guaranteed a fun and exciting read every time!

Look for Marie Ferrarella's upcoming Yours Truly, *Traci on the Spot*, in March 1997.

Here's a special sneak preview....

Morgan Brigham slowly set down his coffee cup on the kitchen table and stared at the comic strip in the center of his paper. It was nestled in among approximately twenty others that were spread out across two pages. But this was the only one he made a point of reading faithfully each morning at breakfast.

This was the only one that mirrored *her* life.

He read each panel twice, as if he couldn't trust his own eyes. But he could. It was there, in black and white.

Morgan folded the paper slowly, thoughtfully, his mind not on his task. So Traci was getting engaged.

The realization gnawed at the lining of his stomach. He hadn't a clue as to why.

He had even less of a clue why he did what he did next.

Abandoning his coffee, now cool, and the newspaper, and ignoring the fact that this was going to make him late for the office, Morgan went to get a sheet of stationery from the den.

He didn't have much time.

Traci Richardson stared at the last frame she had just drawn. Debating, she glanced at the creature sprawled out on the kitchen floor.

"What do you think, Jeremiah? Too blunt?"

The dog, part bloodhound, part mutt, idly looked up from his rawhide bone at the sound of his name. Jeremiah gave her a look she felt free to interpret as ambivalent.

"Fine help you are. What if Daniel actually reads this and puts two and two together?"

Not that there was all that much chance that the man who had proposed to her, the very prosperous and busy Dr. Daniel Thane, would actually see the comic strip she drew for a living. Not unless the strip was taped to a bicuspid he was examining. Lately Daniel had gotten so busy he'd stopped reading anything but the morning headlines of the *Times.*

Still, you never knew. "I don't want to hurt his feelings," Traci continued, using Jeremiah as a sounding board. "It's just that Traci is overwhelmed by Donald's proposal and, see, she thinks the ring is going to swallow her up." To prove her point, Traci held up the drawing for the dog to view.

This time, he didn't even bother to lift his head.

Traci stared moodily at the small velvet box on the kitchen counter. It had sat there since Daniel had asked her to marry him last Sunday. Even if Daniel never read her comic strip, he was going to suspect something eventually. The very fact that she hadn't grabbed the ring from his hand and slid it onto her finger should have told him that she had doubts about their union.

Traci sighed. Daniel was a catch by any definition. So what was her problem? She kept waiting to be struck by that sunny ray of happiness. Daniel said he wanted to take care of her, to fulfill her every wish. And he was even willing to let her think about it before she gave him her answer.

Guilt nibbled at her. She should be dancing up and down, not wavering like a weather vane in a gale.

Pronouncing the strip completed, she scribbled her signature in the corner of the last frame and then sighed. Another week's work put to bed. She glanced at the pile of mail on the counter. She'd been bringing it in steadily from the mailbox since Monday, but the stack had gotten no farther than her kitchen. Sorting letters seemed the least heinous of all the annoying chores that faced her.

Traci paused as she noted a long envelope. Morgan Brigham. Why would Morgan be writing to her?

Curious, she tore open the envelope and quickly scanned the short note inside.

Dear Traci,
I'm putting the summerhouse up for sale. Thought you might want to come up and see it one more time before it goes up on the block. Or make a bid for it yourself. If memory serves, you once said you wanted to buy it. Either way, let me know. My number's on the card.
Take care,
Morgan

P.S. Got a kick out of *Traci on the Spot* this week.

Traci folded the letter. He read her strip. She hadn't known that. A feeling of pride silently coaxed a smile to her lips. After a beat, though, the rest of his note seeped into her consciousness. He was selling the house.

The summerhouse. A faded white building with brick trim. Suddenly, memories flooded her mind. Long, lazy afternoons that felt as if they would never end.

Morgan.

She looked at the far wall in the family room. There was a large framed photograph of her and Morgan standing before the summerhouse. Traci and Morgan. Morgan and

Traci. Back then, it seemed their lives had been permanently intertwined. A bittersweet feeling of loss passed over her.

Traci quickly pulled the telephone over to her on the counter and tapped out the number on the keypad.

*   *   *   *   *

Look for TRACI ON THE SPOT
by Marie Ferrarella, coming to
Silhouette YOURS TRULY
in March 1997.

**In February, Silhouette Books is proud
to present the sweeping, sensual new novel
by bestselling author**

CAIT LONDON

about her unforgettable family—*The Tallchiefs.*

TALLCHIEF FOR KEEPS

Everyone in Amen Flats, Wyoming, was talking about
Elspeth Tallchief. How she wasn't a thirty-three-year-old
virgin, after all. How she'd been keeping herself warm at
night all these years with a couple of secrets. And now one
of those secrets had walked right into town, sending
everyone into a frenzy. But Elspeth knew he'd come for
the *other* secret....

"Cait London is an irresistible storyteller..."
—*Romantic Times*

Don't miss TALLCHIEF FOR KEEPS by Cait London, available
at your favorite retail outlet in February from

Silhouette®

As seen on TV!
Free Gift Offer

With a Free Gift proof-of-purchase from any Silhouette® book,
you can receive a beautiful cubic zirconia pendant.

This gorgeous marquise-shaped stone is a genuine cubic
zirconia—accented by an 18" gold tone necklace.

(Approximate retail value $19.95)

Send for yours today...
compliments of ▼ *Silhouette*®
™

To receive your free gift, a cubic zirconia pendant, send us one original proof-of-purchase, photocopies not accepted, from the back of any Silhouette Romance™, Silhouette Desire®, Silhouette Special Edition®, Silhouette Intimate Moments® or Silhouette Yours Truly™ title available in February, March and April at your favorite retail outlet, together with the Free Gift Certificate, plus a check or money order for $1.65 U.S./$2.15 CAN. (do not send cash) to cover postage and handling, payable to Silhouette Free Gift Offer. We will send you the specified gift. Allow 6 to 8 weeks for delivery. Offer good until April 30, 1997 or while quantities last. Offer valid in the U.S. and Canada only.

Free Gift Certificate

Name: _____

Address: _____

City: _____ State/Province: _____ Zip/Postal Code: _____

Mail this certificate, one proof-of-purchase and a check or money order for postage and handling to: SILHOUETTE FREE GIFT OFFER 1997. In the U.S.: 3010 Walden Avenue, P.O. Box 9077, Buffalo NY 14269-9077. In Canada: P.O. Box 613, Fort Erie, Ontario L2Z 5X3.

FREE GIFT OFFER   084-KFD
ONE PROOF-OF-PURCHASE
To collect your fabulous FREE GIFT, a cubic zirconia pendant, you must include this original proof-of-purchase for each gift with the properly completed Free Gift Certificate.

084-KFD

SILHOUETTE® *Desire*

COMING NEXT MONTH

#1057 TIGHT-FITTIN' JEANS—Mary Lynn Baxter

Garth Dixon, March's *Man of the Month*, had given up on love and marriage, but the way city girl Tiffany Russell looked in her jeans took his breath away. If Garth wasn't careful, he'd find himself escorting her down the aisle!

#1058 THE FIVE-MINUTE BRIDE—Leanne Banks

How To Catch a Princess

Emily St. Clair always dreamed of marrying her own Prince Charming, so she ran away from her wedding into the arms of rough and rugged sheriff Beau Ramsey. If only Beau wasn't so set on his bachelor ways!

#1059 HAVE BRIDE, NEED GROOM—Maureen Child

Jenny Blake needed a husband—fast! She had only four days to get married and stop the family curse. So she risked everything and married reluctant groom Nick Tarantelli for one year's time....

#1060 A BABY FOR MOMMY—Sara Orwig

Micah Drake wasn't certain if the beautiful amnesiac woman he rescued was single and available...or her married twin sister. But one thing was clear—making love to this woman was a risk he was willing to take.

#1061 WEDDING FEVER—Susan Crosby

Maggie Walters's wish to be a bride by her thirtieth birthday finally came true—unfortunately, groom J.D. Duran was marrying her only to protect her. But J.D. soon discovered *he* was the one in danger...of losing his heart.

#1062 PRACTICE HUSBAND—Judith McWilliams

Joe Barrington was not a marrying man. But when Joe found himself teaching his friend Addy Edson how to attract a husband, would Addy's enticing ways lure him into marriage?

Beginning next month from

SILHOUETTE®

Desire®

The Family McCormick

by
Elizabeth Bevarly

Watch as three siblings separated in childhood
are reunited and find love along the way!

ROXY AND THE RICH MAN (D #1053, February 1997)—
Wealthy businessman Spencer Melbourne finds love with the
sexy female detective he hires to find his long-lost twin.

LUCY AND THE LONER (D #1063, April 1997)—
Independent Lucy Dolan shows her gratitude to the fire
fighter who comes to her rescue—by becoming his slave
for a month.

And coming your way in July 1997—
THE FAMILY McCORMICK continues with the wonderful
story of the oldest McCormick sibling. Don't miss any of
these delightful stories. Only from Silhouette Desire.

The spirit of the holidays...
The magic of romance...
They both come together in

You're invited as Merline Lovelace and Carole Buck—
two of your favorite authors from two of your favorite
lines—capture your hearts with five joyous love stories
celebrating the excitement that happens when you
combine holidays and weddings!

Beginning in October, watch for

HALLOWEEN HONEYMOON by Merline Lovelace
(Desire #1030, 10/96)

Thanksgiving—
WRONG BRIDE, RIGHT GROOM by Merline Lovelace
(Desire #1037, 11/96)

Christmas—
A BRIDE FOR SAINT NICK by Carole Buck
(Intimate Moments #752, 12/96)

New Year's Day—
RESOLVED TO (RE)MARRY by Carole Buck
(Desire #1049, 1/97)

Valentine's Day—
THE 14TH...AND FOREVER by Merline Lovelace
(Intimate Moments #764, 2/97)

You're About to Become a *Privileged Woman*

Reap the rewards of fabulous free gifts and benefits with proofs-of-purchase from Silhouette and Harlequin books

Pages & Privileges™

It's our way of thanking you for buying our books at your favorite retail stores.

PROOF OF PURCHASE

SD-PP22

Offer expires March 31, 1997

Pages & Privileges ™

**Harlequin and Silhouette—
the most privileged readers in the world!**

For more information about Harlequin and Silhouette's PAGES & PRIVILEGES program call the Pages & Privileges Benefits Desk: 1-503-794-2499

Silhouette®

SD-PP22